As the two walked home with Friday, Andi told her brother, "We can't send him outside alone anymore. If Friday gets picked up and taken to the pound again, we might not be able to get him out. And it's just going to get harder once school starts." Andi sighed. "I think we need to find a place for Friday to live."

"I've got a few ideas," Bruce offered brightly. "We'll look for a—"

But Andi stopped him. "We've been hiding him in alleys and garages for three years, Bruce," she said. "I think he'd be better off in a *real* home with a *real* family."

DREAMWORKS PICTURES AND NICKELODEON MOVIES
PRESENT

DREAMWORKS PICTURES and NICKELODEON MOVIES
PRESENT

HOTEL FOR DOGS

Movie Novelization

adapted by Erica David
based on the book by Lois Duncan
screenplay by Jeff Lowell and Bob Schooley & Mark McCorkle

Simon Spotlight
New York London Toronto Sydney

SIMON SPOTLIGHT

An imprint of Simon & Schuster Children's Publishing Division

1230 Avenue of the Americas, New York, New York 10020

TM Paramount Pictures. © 2008 DreamWorks LLC. All Rights Reserved.

SIMON SPOTLIGHT and colophon are registered trademarks of Simon & Schuster, Inc.

Manufactured in the United States of America

First Edition 10 9 8 7 6 5 4 3 2

ISBN-13: 978-1-4169-7183-2

ISBN-10: 1-4169-7183-1

Chapter 1

Friday was tied up, the end of his makeshift leash wrapped tightly around a lamppost. It wasn't the first time that the Jack Russell terrier had found himself in this situation, so he sat with his tail thumping on the pavement while he waited patiently for his humans to emerge from a nearby store.

Friday would have been content to keep waiting if it hadn't been for the man down the street—the one holding the world's most delicious-smelling hot dog. Friday could hardly ignore the scent. And he had no choice but to follow his nose.

So, as he had done many times before, the little

terrier shook his head back and forth until the leash loosened around his neck. Ducking his head, he flattened his ears and carefully crawled out of the leash. Ah, sweet freedom!

Friday followed the scent of the hot dog down the busy city street, dodging pedestrians, baby strollers, and bikes, with a single-minded purpose: *Hot dog. Now.*

At last Friday reached his goal. The hot dog was in the hand of a man sitting on a bench. There was just one bite of the hot dog left, and Friday knew what he had to do. He sat up on his hind legs, stared at the man with the saddest expression he could muster, and started to whimper.

"Aw, what's the matter, doggie? You want some?" the man asked. He held the hot dog out to Friday and waved it right under his nose. As soon as Friday moved to take a bite, the man snatched the hot dog away! Friday barked in frustration.

Just then a large truck rumbled down the street and roared through a puddle in front of the bench, spraying the man with water. Friday saw his chance. He jumped up, snatched the last bite of the hot dog, and swallowed it in one satisfying gulp. Then he scampered away, leaving the wet and angry man to sulk behind him.

After all, it wasn't every day that a dog taught a human how to behave.

"Hurry up!" Andi said. Her little brother, Bruce, was taking way too much time in the bathroom, as usual.

"Almost done!" the eleven-year-old called through the door. Bruce rummaged through his backpack in the tiny public restroom. He pulled out a rock and tested its weight in his hand. Nah, too heavy, he thought. He reached in to pick another rock. This one was too light. He felt like Goldilocks as he searched for the rock that was just right.

"What is taking so long?" Andi hissed.

"This is a delicate process!" Bruce replied just as he found the perfect rock. He dropped it into an empty cell-phone box and sifted through his backpack again. This time he pulled out a large sheet of thin, clear plastic. Bruce placed the sheet on top of the box, held the entire thing under the hand dryer, and punched the button.

The dryer roared to life, and the hot air caused the plastic to shrink tight around the cell-phone box. *Voilà!* Instant shrink-wrap.

"I'm done!" Bruce said. He opened the door and tossed

the box to his sixteen-year-old sister. Catching it easily, Andi tucked the box under her arm and headed for the pawnshop on the corner as Bruce crossed his fingers.

When Andi reached the pawnshop, she took a deep breath and closed her eyes for a moment. People will believe anything you tell them as long as you say it with confidence, she reminded herself.

A guy wearing a leather jacket and a cap walked up to the pawnshop. Andi quickly figured he was the perfect mark. She watched him enter the store and then strolled in after him.

Inside the shop Andi waited until the guy looked her way, then she tossed him a sweet smile and walked up to the counter.

"Do you buy, like, electronic stuff?" Andi asked the pawnbroker.

The old man glanced over his shoulder at the rows of electronic devices behind him. It was clearly a stupid question.

"Duh. Helloooo," Andi said as she followed his gaze. Then she started her spiel. "So, I've got this cell phone. I never even opened it. See? It's still shrink-wrapped and everything. It cost me two hundred dollars, and I need to sell it."

The pawnbroker was not moved. "Take it back where you bought it," he said blandly.

Andi continued, "I bought it with cash, I mislaid the receipt, and then right after I got home I got a call that I lost my job because I forgot to . . . go. Anyway, I really can't afford it anymore. I'll sell it to you for a hundred."

The store owner stared at her for a moment. Andi fought the urge to chew her lip. She looked back at the guy in the leather jacket, hoping for some sympathy. Finally the pawnbroker took the box from her.

"Are you even eighteen?" he asked.

"Of course!" she answered. "I'm flattered you asked, though. You made my day. Wait until I tell my kids."

The pawnbroker frowned. Andi knew she'd gone too far with that last remark about the kids. "I'm sixteen . . . ," she confessed. "But I'm almost eighteen."

Shaking his head, the pawnbroker handed the cell-phone box back to her. Andi gave an exasperated sigh and turned to leave, but not before glancing back to see if the guy had taken the bait.

She got her answer a moment later when he followed her outside the store.

"You mind if I take a look?" he asked.

Andi shrugged and handed him the cell-phone box.

11

The guy looked at the box for a moment and came to a decision.

"I'll give you twenty bucks for it," he offered.

"Done," Andi said. Score one for confidence.

"So, how'd we do?" Bruce asked when Andi met up with him later.

"Twenty dollars," Andi replied.

"Nobody questions the shrink-wrap," Bruce said with satisfaction.

They walked toward the lamppost to find Friday waiting for them. After the hot dog, he had cleaned up a Popsicle dropped by a toddler, found a half-eaten banana, and begged for potato chips from a girl. Little did his humans know what he'd really been up to.

When Bruce reached down to untie him, he noticed that the dog's collar had slipped off. The siblings were impressed. "And he waited right here," Andi said. "What a good boy."

Friday happily wagged his tail. Good boy, indeed!

The three of them went to the park. Bruce fed Friday several cheeseburgers and watched in amazement as he wolfed them all down.

"Is it normal for an animal to be able to consume ten percent of its body weight in one meal?" Andi asked.

"It happens, but usually after they do it, they hibernate for six months," Bruce replied.

Friday finished his meal and turned expectantly to Andi and Bruce. Bruce looked from Friday to his own cheeseburger and back to Friday again.

Andi scratched the top of Friday's head, just behind the ears. "Do you have any idea what we go through to fill your bottomless pit?" she asked.

Friday barked.

"I think that's a yes," Bruce said as he reluctantly tore off a piece of his cheeseburger and tossed it to his dog.

Suddenly Andi jumped up. "Uh-oh, here comes trouble." The guy who bought the "phone" was headed their way—and this time he had company in the form of a stern-looking police officer.

"This can't be good," Bruce croaked.

Andi quickly issued a sharp command to Friday: "Go!"

The dog hurried off to hide. Bruce wanted to do the same, but he wasn't quick enough. He fumbled with his backpack as the police officer got closer and closer.

Andi, on the other hand, knew that there was only one way out of the situation. She picked up her bag and walked straight toward the two men.

"Excuse me, miss, I'm Officer Mike. Could I talk to you over here?" the policeman said just as Andi approached.

"Me?" Andi asked, doing her best impression of the world's coolest cucumber.

"That's her. She's the one who ripped me off," the guy said.

"What? I've never seen this guy before in my life," Andi lied. She didn't like to think of it as lying, though. It was more like stretching the truth or at least kneading it a bit between her sweaty palms.

"She's lying. She's the one who ran the scam."

"This guy again," Andi said. "Thank goodness you're here, officer. He's been stalking me all day. I'm a little freaked out."

Officer Mike regarded her carefully, not buying her story at all. Confidence, Andi reminded herself. But that was before Bruce ran smack into a second police officer.

"Hey Mike, get a load of this," the other officer said, pointing to Bruce—and spilling everything out of his backpack.

"What do we have here?" Officer Mike asked his partner, as several rocks, sheets of plastic, and an empty iPod box fell onto the ground.

"That's pretty weird, huh?" Bruce said, trying to sound innocent.

Andi made one last-ditch effort to turn things around. "Those are for my brother's arts and crafts project."

But Officer Mike was not convinced. "Oh, yeah?" he said. "Well, this just might be the first time arts and crafts ever landed anybody in jail."

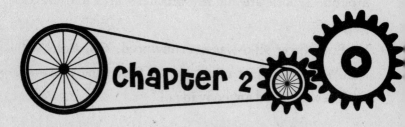

Chapter 2

Bernie Wilkins couldn't believe it. Here it was dinnertime, and instead of being home with his lovely wife, Carol, he was standing in a police station—a familiar police station.

Bernie walked up to the front desk and shook hands with the sergeant on duty.

"Thanks for calling, George," he said.

Behind his desk George shrugged. "Either I call you or I fill out a lot of forms."

"I hear that," Bernie replied. "So, where are they?"

George nodded to where Andi and Bruce sat on a bench in front of a holding cell. "We didn't actually put them behind bars," he told the social worker.

Bernie sighed. "Maybe you should have," he said. "It might have scared some sense into them."

"Hey, Bernie," Bruce and Andi said as he walked up to them.

"Don't 'hey' me," Bernie replied. "You know what I was doing when my phone rang? Explaining to my wife that I wouldn't let work ruin tonight."

"We're sorry," Andi said.

"Sorry for what? Sorry you got caught? Sorry for what you did? Or sorry you made me come down here in the middle of my dinner?"

"All of the above?" Bruce suggested.

"Smart kid. So I shouldn't have to remind you that I'm your social worker, not your bail bondsman."

"Of course not, Bernie," Andi said. "But I really think you're missing the point. I'm the victim here. That guy was trying to rip off a poor innocent girl."

"You sold him a rock in a box for twenty bucks."

Andi laughed.

"You know what? This is anything but funny," Bernie said firmly.

"'A rock in a box for twenty bucks.' It sounds like a Dr. Seuss con," answered Andi.

17

"Andi, this is serious. What if they'd called Carl and Lois Scudder instead of me?"

Andi shrugged. "I guess you'd have to find new foster parents for us then."

Bernie looked at her. *So that's what this is about: They are unhappy with their latest foster parents.*

"Don't play that game, Andi," Bernie warned, but his voice was gentle. "Because it's a dangerous game. I don't think you understand how hard it is to find a place for the two of you."

"They're only taking care of us for the check from the government," Andi said.

"And the free labor," Bruce added.

"Chores aren't free labor," Bernie explained.

"Since when is grouting a chore?" Andi asked. "I'm just glad they live in an apartment instead of a house or else they'd figure out a way to have us retile the roof."

Bernie's patience was wearing thin. "What did you really use the money on?"

"Edible food," Andi answered.

Bernie smirked in spite of himself.

"It's true," Bruce insisted. "You haven't eaten Lois's cooking. Trust me. We're all starving."

"All?" Bernie asked, his eyebrow arched in curiosity.

"All both of us," Andi covered smoothly.

"Well, come on all both of you. It's time to take you home."

When they got to the front door of the Scudders' apartment, the three of them were greeted with a horrible wailing noise coming from inside. "Let me guess," Bernie said. "Band practice?"

While the noise inside the apartment grew louder, Andi reached into her bag to find her keys. She winced as she heard Carl and Lois begin to sing—if you could call it that. The sound was one part nails on a chalkboard and two parts angry cat, the combination of which was simply ear-splitting. And then the couple started an argument that was as loud as the music.

"You know, Lois, the word 'harmonizing' comes from the word 'harmony,'" Carl told his wife.

"So?" Lois said.

"I'm saying that you're still half a step off."

"A half step off?" Lois asked. "It's funny that my vocal instructor, who's a *paid* vocal instructor, doesn't notice that, but you do."

"Here's the note," Carl replied, hoping to dispel the nagging thought that occurred to him every time they practiced: that his wife was tone deaf. He plucked the note on his guitar, and Lois tried to repeat it. Andi was sure that Lois would never be on key, but Carl just couldn't leave it alone. He kept plucking the note more and more insistently, and Lois kept singing more and more insistently. They went on this way for another minute or so. *Pluck*. SING. *Pluck*. SING.

Andi realized she couldn't put it off any longer and opened the door. She looked from Carl, with his tie-dyed T-shirt and scraggly, shoulder-length brown hair, to Lois, with her ratty blond locks and shiny red leather pants. Somehow the two of them had the idea that they had what it took to form a rock band; theirs was called the Carl Scudder Experience. It didn't matter that they weren't particularly talented or that they were perhaps a little too old to be in a rock band. When it came to murdering music, they were unstoppable.

Lois finally noticed Andi and broke off from the pluck-sing showdown. "You're late," she said tersely, "and you're interrupting rehearsal."

"Sorry," Andi mumbled.

"Your food's on your trays," Lois said, pointing to two TV tray tables with plates of what may have once been edible but was now a goopy gray mess after Lois had "cooked" it.

"Yummy," Andi said sarcastically. "Too bad we already ate."

"Fine. It'll be lunch tomorrow," Lois replied.

Andi made a face just as Bernie and Bruce walked up beside her.

"Hey, Bernie," Carl greeted the social worker. "Didn't you say you have a friend who owns a club?"

"Still don't, Carl," Bernie replied.

"Okay. Cool. Right. Yeah. Cool," Carl said.

"Excuse me, but can we focus on the issue at hand?" Lois asked. Everyone turned to look at her. "I'm a kind woman. In fact, people are always saying to me, 'Lois, why are you so kind?' But you two know the rules: We serve dinner at a certain time so we can finish dinner at a certain time so we can rehearse at a certain time—"

"So we can drop our rock manifesto on the world at a certain time," Carl finished.

Lois rolled her eyes. "Those times have come and gone, Carl." Then she turned to Bernie and asked, "Now, where were they?"

Andi and Bruce quickly glanced at Bernie. If he told the Scudders that she and Bruce had spent the better part of the afternoon at the police station, they'd be in deep trouble.

"Truth is, it's my fault," Bernie said. "I just wanted to catch up with them, and we were having so much fun that I lost track of time. You have my apologies. Now, why don't I take them back to their room so you can continue making the magic?"

The Scudders seemed satisfied with Bernie's answer and went back to making music.

When they were in their room, Andi said, "Thanks for covering for us, Bernie."

Bernie shook his head. "You two can't afford to screw this up," he insisted. "You haven't even been here two months. They're your fifth set of foster parents in three years."

"The Johnsons don't count. We were only there for two hours," Bruce said.

"Do you know what the reaction is when I tell people I want to place eleven- and sixteen-year-old sibs?" Bernie said, exasperated.

Andi and Bruce didn't answer. They liked Bernie and knew that he cared about them. They were sorry about what they put him through.

"If you screw this up, there are no more favors I can call in," Bernie added. "I'm going to have to place you separately."

"No, you know that's not the plan, Bernie," Andi protested. "We stay together."

"Well, if you want to stay together, you have to make this work." Bernie looked at the two of them. They were good kids. He didn't mean to be harsh; he really just wanted what was best for them. "I'm going to share a little trick I've learned. When someone is telling me something I don't want to hear, I smile and nod. I even throw in a 'hmm' once in a while. Works wonders. Got it?"

"Hmm," Andi and Bruce replied with a smile and a nod.

Bernie smiled. "Nice. Okay, we're done, but I don't want to get a phone call about a trick with a brick or a scam with a ham." The siblings burst out laughing; then Bernie and Bruce did their special signature handshake before the social worker left.

Alone again in their small room, Andi and Bruce sat in silence for a moment. At least they had a place to keep a couple of the things that mattered most to them. One of those things was a picture of their family taken just before they'd lost their parents. The other thing stood on the fire escape outside their window, with his cold, wet nose pressed to the glass.

Bruce got up and opened the window. Friday hopped over the sill and into the room. He licked their faces in delight.

"Thank goodness it's Friday," Bruce said.

Chapter 3

When Bruce woke up the next morning, he had a strange feeling that something was wrong. He sat up in bed and looked around. At first glance everything seemed normal. Andi was still asleep in her bed across from him, but something was missing.

Then it hit him—and Bruce sprang out of bed. "Andi, wake up!" he said. "Friday's gone!"

The window was closed, so the siblings knew there was only one place Friday could have wandered off to, and that was the kitchen—Lois's domain.

Lois was busy in the kitchen, banging pots and pans and trying to figure out what to cook. She had not noticed Friday nosing around. He had managed to grab a bit of sausage and a piece of bread while Lois's back was turned.

Andi and Bruce rushed in just as Friday hopped down from the counter. Lois was locking one of her food cabinets. Much to her frustration, the kids seemed to always be hungry and expecting to be fed, and she couldn't have them finding her food that was actually edible.

"Good morning!" Andi yelled, hoping to distract Lois.

"Stop shouting!" Lois yelled back, startled. "What are you two doing up so early?"

"We thought we'd get some breakfast!" Bruce replied, a little too cheerfully. He had just seen Friday's tail wag beneath the kitchen table.

"Calm down, will you? The cereal's in the unlocked cupboard. You know how to get it."

"Oh, but that egglike thing you're making looks so good," Andi said.

"Too bad," Lois replied. "I am not your servant. I'm obligated to give you two meals a day and that's lunch and dinner. You know the deal."

At that moment Friday decided to hop onto a

chair, using it to reach the counter and the top of the refrigerator.

Bruce watched in terror as the little dog almost knocked a bottle off of the fridge. It would have landed on Lois.

"Friday!" he shouted.

"What?" Lois asked.

"I said, what's the day after Thursday?" Andi said, thinking quickly.

"Friday!" Bruce repeated.

"Thank you!" Andi replied.

"What is the matter with you two?" Lois asked. The kids were definitely testing her patience.

"We're just excited to be here!" Bruce answered as Friday continued to sniff around the kitchen until he found a plate of bacon. Jackpot!

It took some effort, but Andi managed to get Lois's attention by telling her a made-up story. Bruce then quietly wrangled Friday away from the food. He scooped the dog in his arms and held him behind his back as they made their way out of the kitchen. The two were almost home free when Lois shouted, "Wait! What are you up to, mister?"

"Just . . . heading to my room," Bruce replied nervously.

"I'll come with you!" Andi said, and the two of them stumbled out of the kitchen.

Lois shook her head, sure that the kids were up to no good, but she had no time right now to find out what that was.

As soon as they reached their room, Bruce and Andi let Friday out onto the fire escape outside their window. It was way too risky keeping him inside, especially when there was food around.

Friday padded down the fire escape and jumped down to the sidewalk. He sniffed once, twice, and then found the scent he was looking for. It didn't matter that he had just filled up on bacon from Lois's kitchen. There was always room in his stomach for more.

Trotting down the street, Friday spotted a shiny silver vending cart that was the source of the mouthwatering smell. The cart was on the move, and Friday eagerly followed.

Friday stepped up his pace as he let the delicious scent guide him—right into a large, burly man who stood over him holding a dog-catching loop.

"You make it too easy," the man said with a smirk.

Later that afternoon Bruce and Andi were out looking for Friday; it was not like him to miss a meal.

Bruce cranked the handle of one of his favorite inventions, a can opener attached to an amplifying horn from an old-fashioned record player. The whole thing was hooked up to a small electric motor with a hand crank. Each time Bruce turned the crank, the sound of the can opener was broadcast throughout the neighborhood. It was Bruce's version of a dinner bell.

"Maybe Friday can't hear it," Andi said.

"It's mealtime. He could hear it on the moon," Bruce retorted.

Their search led them past an old brownstone with a fenced-in yard, where a big, mean-looking dog raced toward the fence. He wore a spiked choke collar attached to a thick chain, and he was snarling. Andi and Bruce jumped back, but just as the dog reached the fence, he flopped down in front of them and panted happily.

"Aw, he's just lonely," Bruce said, reaching out a hand for the dog to sniff.

"Bruce, don't," Andi warned, but it was too late. The dog took one sniff and knew that he liked Bruce immediately. He licked the boy's fingers, as an old man stepped out of the brownstone.

"Get away from him!" the man shouted angrily.

"Sorry," Bruce apologized, as he and Andi both took a quick step back.

The man started scolding his dog. "You're worthless! Bark at them! You're supposed to guard me!" He jerked roughly at the dog's chain.

"Your dog needs water," Bruce said, but the man ignored him.

"Come on, Bruce," Andi said, pulling him away from the fence.

Andi and Bruce continued searching for Friday, but after another hour had passed, they were beginning to get worried. They'd been all over the neighborhood, and there was still no sign of Friday. It was time to start asking around. At the end of the block they came to a small grocery store called Camwell's Market, where a teenage boy was hosing down the sidewalk.

"Excuse me," Andi said. "Have you seen a cute little dog around here?"

The boy turned and looked at Andi. "No, but I see a fox," he answered with a grin. "Name's Mark."

Andi rolled her eyes. "He's white and he's got brown ears," she said, ignoring his comment.

"Wait, something's coming to me," Mark said. "Little

dog. White with brown ears, right?"

Before Andi could respond, the store owner, Mrs. Camwell, stepped out of the store, and she didn't look too friendly.

"You—keep your dog on a leash," Mrs. Camwell said sternly to Andi. "And you—hose the muck," she told Mark.

Andi didn't need to be told twice. She and Bruce hurried away as Mark called out, "Hey, you should probably give me your phone number in case I see your dog . . ."

Andi didn't bother to turn around.

"Or just come back and find me here. I like your style," Mark added.

By late afternoon Andi and Bruce were beginning to panic. They had gone back to the apartment to make up some flyers with Friday's photo, and now they were scouring the neighborhood in earnest. They stopped at Primary Paws, a pet store and grooming salon.

The store was busy, and there was a small crowd gathered around a table of adorable puppies. Bruce began to hand out flyers while Andi looked for someone who worked there. She spotted a girl about her own age wearing an apron and a name tag that read HEATHER.

Heather had just finished trimming and grooming a small Pomeranian and was carrying it to the back of the store. Heather loved her job, loved animals, and loved her coworker, Dave.

"Nice haircut," Dave said as Heather passed by.

"Thanks, Dave, I was hoping you'd notice," Heather replied, blushing.

"Oh, I actually meant the Pomeranian," he teased. Then he noticed Andi and Bruce at the front of the store. "Can I help you?" he asked.

"Yes," Andi said, handing Dave a flyer. "We're looking for our dog. I don't suppose you've seen him?"

"Friday," he read. "That's an interesting name. Where'd that come from?"

"It's a long story," Andi answered.

"Got it. Hey, I don't think I've seen you before. Do you go to Thomas Jefferson?" Dave asked.

"Uh, I will this fall. My family just moved here a couple of months ago," Andi said, forcing a smile to cover up the reality of her life.

"How do you like it so far?" Dave asked.

"What's not to like?"

Bruce cut his sister a look. This was not getting-to-know-you time. Friday was missing!

32

"We should get going," Andi said quickly.

"Okay. Good luck finding your dog," Dave replied, unaware that Heather had been watching him the whole time.

"Your tongue's hanging out, boy," Heather said.

Dave jumped. *Busted!* he thought to himself.

"Oh, actually I meant the Pomeranian," she added slyly.

chapter 4

The cold gray stone buildings of the City Pound loomed large in front of them. Neither sibling wanted to be there, but they felt that they didn't have a choice. It was the only place they hadn't checked.

Bruce swallowed hard. "It looks like a prison," he said grimly.

Andi nodded. The place gave her the creeps too.

Inside, rows of metal cages were stacked from floor to ceiling like jail cells. Each cell had its own canine inmate, looking desperate to be freed. The dogs paced, howled, and barked. Bruce and Andi could barely look at them.

They trudged toward the front desk with their flyers, just as an Animal Control employee walked in with a small white terrier snagged in his dog-catching loop. He was headed for one of the cages.

"It's Friday!" Bruce yelled.

"That's him—that's our dog!" Andi called to the dogcatcher, who stopped and looked from the kids to the dog. He pointed to Friday as if to ask 'Is this yours'? Bruce and Andi eagerly nodded, sure that the man would simply hand Friday over to them.

But the dogcatcher smirked and then put Friday in a cage, slamming the door loudly before locking it.

Andi stepped up to a guy at the front desk. He was holding one of her flyers about Friday.

"He just came in," said the man, whose name tag identified him as JAKE.

"We know; we just saw him," Andi said hopefully.

"I love it when these stories have a happy ending," Jake said without enthusiasm. "Well, we're open until six, so just bring your parents in and—"

Andi's heart sank. "Parents? Wait, no. I mean, is that really necessary? We're already here and that's our dog—"

"Listen, kid, there's a whole thing with paperwork,

and I am not about to go screwing up the paperwork. That is *not* who I am," Jake said firmly.

While Andi pleaded with Jake, Bruce looked around the pound. It was definitely overcrowded, but at least the dogs seemed to be fed regularly, and they sort of had each other for company. If anything, the pound was a warm place to sleep on a cold night. Maybe, just maybe, it wasn't such a prison after all.

Bruce began to relax a little. But what he saw a few seconds later made him panic. An Animal Control guy was struggling as he led a dog down a long hallway toward a door marked "13." When he came out a short while later, the employee came out of the room holding nothing but an empty leash.

It was then that Bruce noticed the sign: CHECK FOR YOUR LOST DOG EVERY DAY! WE CAN ONLY HOLD ANIMALS FOR 72 HOURS! It didn't take a genius to figure out what happened if no one claimed the dogs.

He tugged on Andi's sleeve and pointed at the sign. She read it quickly and turned back to Jake.

"All right," she told him. "I'm going to level with you. That dog means everything to us. We've had him for a long time, and I honestly don't know what we'd do if anything happened to him. My parents aren't coming in. If I told you the real reason why, I'd start crying, you'd start crying, and it would be a big, miserable mess. So I'm going to give you every penny I have in the world and you're going to look the other way and let that dog out."

Andi dug into her bag and put all the money she had down on the desk.

Jake looked at her for a moment. "I'm only doing this because I'm a good guy," he said before grabbing the money and stuffing it into his pocket.

As the two walked home with Friday, Andi told her brother, "We can't send him outside alone anymore. If Friday gets picked up and taken to the pound again, we might not be able to get him out. And it's just going to get harder once school starts." Andi sighed. "I think we need to find a place for Friday to live."

"I've got a few ideas," Bruce offered brightly. "We'll look for a—"

But Andi stopped him. "We've been hiding him in alleys and garages for three years, Bruce," she said. "I think he'd be better off in a *real* home with a *real* family."

"We *are* a real family," Bruce insisted. Just then they were startled by a loud noise. A group of kids ran past them and disappeared into an alley, followed by a police car. As it rounded the corner, its headlights shined right at Andi and Bruce.

They immediately took off down the street, with Friday leading the way.

"Hold on up there!" a police officer called out. He and his partner jumped out of the car and began to run after them.

Andi, Bruce, and Friday raced down another alley, dodging Dumpsters and old cardboard boxes. They could hear the officers' footsteps gaining on them. Turning right at the end of the alley, they found themselves face-to-face with a monstrous old building. Friday darted through a small crack in one of the doors.

The siblings hesitated. The place looked abandoned, with most of the windows on the ground floor boarded up. A dilapidated sign hung crookedly over the delivery entrance. It read HOTEL FRANCIS DUKE.

"Friday!" Bruce called.

The officers' footsteps grew louder and louder—they had apparently split up and were closing in from both directions. "Did he have to pick the creepiest building in the alley?" Bruce asked, as he grabbed his sister and pulled her through one of the doors of the old hotel.

As soon as the door closed behind them, they were cloaked in darkness. They held their breaths as they listened to the police officers outside. After a while there was complete silence.

"Let's just find Friday and get out of here," Andi said.

Bruce found a small flashlight in his backpack. When he flipped it on, the two saw that they were in a long, dusty hallway.

Bruce and Andi walked cautiously down the hall. It led them to a large open area cluttered with all kinds of stuff, from worn furniture to old books and newspapers. The walls were covered with tarp and scaffolding, as if someone had once tried to fix the place up.

The siblings picked their way carefully across the room to avoid bumping into giant stacks of cardboard boxes and statues covered in dust. Bruce glanced up at the huge cobweb-covered glass chandeliers above them.

At the end of the room was a long staircase leading up to a second-floor balcony.

"This must have been the lobby—," Bruce started to say, but a strange noise interrupted him. "Did you hear that?"

They stood quietly for several minutes. When they didn't hear anything else, Andi was reassured. "See? It's just an old hotel," she said before a series of thuds began.

"Those are footsteps," Bruce suggested nervously. "Hotels don't make footsteps. People make footsteps. When they walk through hotels. With their *feet*."

"You make a good point," Andi said, inching closer to Bruce. *Who else was in the hotel?* she wondered.

Suddenly something darted in front of the flashlight beam. Bruce tracked the object with the light—and saw the shadow of a huge animal!

Andi covered her mouth to stifle a scream, but as the beast leaped over to them, they saw it was a tiny black-and-white Boston terrier with perky ears and a sweet face! Andi heaved a sigh of relief—until a giant hungry-looking mastiff appeared.

Friday raced out of the darkness.

"Friday!" Bruce yelled, happy to see his dog again.

"Watch out!" Andi called, not sure how the other two dogs would react to Friday.

But there was no cause for concern. All the dogs wagged their tails as they greeted each other. It looked like a reunion of old friends.

After the happy salutations, the dogs scampered up the lobby stairs.

"Do you think they belong to anyone?" Bruce asked as they followed the dogs.

"If they did, would they be here?" Andi said.

"Better here than at the pound."

The mastiff led them to one of the guest rooms on the second floor. There wasn't much in the room, except for a king-size bed. The mastiff jumped up onto the bed, followed by Friday. Then the Boston terrier hopped up and found a cozy spot between the two larger dogs. It was as if they had been friends their whole lives.

Bruce and Andi could hardly believe their eyes. "What about just leaving Friday with them tonight?" Bruce asked. He had a good feeling about this place.

"Well . . . he won't be lonely," Andi answered. It would be better than leaving him alone outside where he could be picked up by Animal Control. "One night."

Andi walked over to the window and pulled down the dusty old shade. When she turned back, the dogs were already fast asleep. It looked like Friday had decided he was going to stay.

Andi and Bruce walked quietly out of the room.

"Good night, guys," Bruce whispered.

chapter 5

The next morning Bernie was getting ready for work while his wife, Carol, was talking to him about something. He was doing his best to listen, but he just couldn't concentrate. He was too busy thinking about Andi and Bruce.

"It's supposed to be a teacher appreciation lunch," Carol said. "And yet it ends up being more work for us by the time we set it up and clean it up. Sometimes I'd like a little less appreciation, you know?"

"Hmm," Bernie said. He nodded and smiled.

"Don't nod and 'hmm' me," Carol snapped. "*I* showed *you* the nod and 'hmm'."

"I'd like to think I've made it my own," he joked.

"Seriously, what's wrong?" Carol asked.

"Those kids. Last night."

"Andi and Bruce? Are they okay?"

"I don't know." Bernie sighed. "It's bad enough that they lost their parents, but if they can't make this one work, I don't know who's going to take them both." Carol put her hands on Bernie's shoulders and turned him around to face her.

"You do everything you can for them," she said softly. "You can't bring your work home and let it make you crazy."

"You're right," Bernie said. "The unfair thing is that they really are good kids."

At that same moment across town, those "good kids" were raiding Lois Scudder's kitchen. Bruce had picked the locks on the cabinets, and he and Andi were now dumping as much food as they could find into their bags. When the cabinets were empty, they moved on to the refrigerator.

Bruce looked up from the armful of lunch meat he had just grabbed to see Lois staring at him.

"Quite a load you got there," she remarked.

Andi winced at the sound of Lois's voice. They were so busted. "Just getting a little breakfast," she said cheerfully.

"You feeding the whole neighborhood?" Lois asked.

Just a few hungry dogs, Bruce thought.

"If I don't eat, you're angry, and if I do eat, you're angry," Andi said.

"Fine, so eat. Lucky for you, I saved your dinners. You can start with those." Lois took two foil-wrapped plates from the refrigerator. She pulled the foil from the plates to reveal what at one time may have been a stew of some sort. It was now a semisolid gray mass. "Go ahead. All of it. Let's go."

Andi and Bruce set down their bags and reluctantly moved toward the plates on the kitchen table. Bruce held his plate up to his nose and sniffed. One whiff and the stale odor made him shrink back in disgust.

At that moment a slow, sad howl cut through the quiet of the morning. Bruce thought it might have been his stomach screaming out in protest, but then he realized that the sound was coming from a dog.

"What is that?" Lois asked.

Andi and Bruce exchanged a quick look. They knew

that they had to get away as quickly as they could. And there was only one way that Lois would let them go. They began shoving the gray masses into their mouths. Andi gagged. It was beyond gross. She didn't know how she was going to clean her plate.

The howling continued. Satisfied the kids were eating, Lois turned away and started making her morning coffee. Andi and Bruce quickly dumped the rest of the dinners into Bruce's backpack. When Lois turned back, Andi and Bruce were smiling at her.

"All done," Andi said, showing her clean plate.

"If you'd just eat the meals I make, you wouldn't get so hungry in the morning."

"You're right. Thank you so much," Andi said as she and Bruce grabbed their bags and ran out of the kitchen.

The plaintive howling continued and grew even louder as the two got closer to the hotel. Finally they sneaked inside through the delivery entrance.

Racing up the stairs, they came to the room where they'd left Friday the night before. There they found the mastiff howling sadly as he stared at the window shade.

"What's the problem?" Bruce asked.

45

"Why are you asking me?" Andi replied, as she turned back to the sad dog and followed his gaze. He was still staring at the shade.

Andi walked over to the window and raised the shade. The howling stopped. She lowered it. The dog howled. She raised the shade. *Silence.* She lowered the shade. *Howl.* Finally Andi left the shade up, and the mastiff grew quiet, happily looking out the window.

"That's it?" she asked. "All so you could look out the window?"

Bruce shook his head. He walked over to Andi and started to pull down the shade again.

"You're going to set him off," Andi said.

"But if we leave the shade up, someone's going to see him."

"Well, there has to be something we can do—some sort of compromise."

Bruce thought for a moment, then looked around the room. "I have an idea," he noted, after spotting a glass lampshade. Bruce closed the window shade, and the howling began again. "Just bear with me, buddy."

Bruce poked a hole in the closed shade with a pen. The hole was enough to let a small beam of light through. Next, he took the lampshade and hung it in front of the light so that it focused the beam. Now, with the lampshade acting as a lens, it projected the view from the window onto the opposite wall of the room, although the view was now upside down.

Andi helped Bruce turn the mastiff around so that he faced the upside-down view. As soon as the dog saw the image on the wall, he stopped howling and settled down.

"How'd you do that?" Andi asked, impressed.

"Camera obscura," he said simply. "The small hole makes the light rays converge and then in an almost prismlike—"

"Stop. If I don't understand the first ten words, it's not going to get better if you keep talking." Andi smiled at him. "Nice work. Smart."

"Thanks," Bruce said.

Andi and Bruce took the dogs down to the lobby to feed them. While Bruce unloaded food from his backpack, Andi poked around the hotel's old check-in desk. Finding an old guest registry marked "HFD," Andi blew the dust off the book, then began to read the faded names of the guests who had once stayed at the hotel.

Bruce laid out several of Lois's meals in front of the dogs. Friday knew not to bother, but the other two dogs moved in to investigate—and quickly shied away after just one sniff.

"Wow, even Lenny and Georgia won't eat it," Bruce observed. "We need to get them some real dog food."

"Wait, *who*?" Andi asked, setting down the registry.

"That's what I named the new dogs."

"No," Andi said. "No naming them. If you name them, you get attached."

"Come on, Andi, look at her. Tell me she's not a Georgia." Bruce pointed to the Boston terrier, who responded by scampering over to lick his fingers.

Andi watched her brother. "Bruce, I'm not kidding," she said. "It's great that Friday likes . . . dog number one and dog number two, but we're barely keeping *our* dog safe. You know what happens if we get caught in here? Trespassing, breaking and entering. Bernie wasn't kidding. They're going to split us up and ship us off."

But Bruce wasn't paying attention to Andi. He was watching Friday, who had dragged one of his favorite toys from Bruce's backpack, a small, patchwork pillow with the words BONE, SWEET BONE stitched on the front. Friday sat on his pillow in the middle of the lobby, panting happily. He couldn't look more at home.

"Are you listening to me?" Andi asked impatiently.

Bruce looked from Friday to his sister and gave her a hopeful smile. He wasn't quite as good at begging as Friday was, but he stared at Andi with his best puppy-dog face.

Andi sighed. Bruce was cheating. Those were doggy tactics, and they won her over every time. "Okay, fine," she said, then added, "for now."

Bruce grinned. "So I'll stay here and keep them quiet while you go for some real food. Okay?"

"I'll be back," Andi said, turning to leave. Then she noticed that Friday and . . . dog number one were following her.

"Stay, Friday," she commanded. "Stay, . . . Georgia."

chapter 6

At Primary Paws, Heather was up to her elbows in suds. She prided herself on her dog-bathing skills and was sure that in a matter of minutes the playful puppy in front of her would be squeaky clean. There was just one small problem: Heather had developed a wicked itch on her nose.

Heather drew one hand out of the bath and gently scratched her nose. Instant relief, but now there were soapsuds on her nose. She tried to brush them off but only succeeded in adding more bubbles.

Heather let go of the dog to reach for a towel. And that was the moment the dog had been waiting for.

He shook himself vigorously, soaking Heather in the process.

"Hey, *you're* the one who needs a bath, not *me*!" Heather exclaimed. With soap bubbles in her eyes, she couldn't see a thing, but she did hear the front door open.

"Hi! How can I help you?" she called out.

Andi picked up a towel and wiped Heather's eyes. Heather blinked a few times and smiled. "Thanks for the hand. Did you find Friday?" she asked.

"Wow, good memory," Andi said.

"Are you kidding? Your dog is Friday, you moved here a few months ago, and you're going to Thomas Jefferson this fall. Your name is Andi, you never said your brother's name, and I'm not being judgmental, but those are the same jeans and shoes you had on the other day."

Andi was speechless.

"My teachers say I have a photographic memory," Heather continued. "I actually remember being born. It was amazing."

"That's cool. So where's the dog food?" Andi asked.

"Um, I forgot," Heather joked as she pointed to a nearby aisle.

Andi walked over to look at the dog food. Everything was so expensive! She pulled out a few crumpled bills from her pocket. This was not good.

The bell on the front door rang, and Andi looked up to see Dave enter the store.

"Hey. I guess you found your dog," Dave said.

"Yeah. He's fine."

"Great. Can I help you with anything?"

"No, just getting some food." Andi checked the price on a large bag of dog food and grimaced.

"That's eighty pounds," Dave said helpfully.

"That's probably right."

"For that little dog on the flyer?"

Uh-oh. Andi quickly searched her brain for a suitable lie. "No, the thing is . . . actually, I have three dogs. The other two are strays that we took in. My parents love animals."

"That's great."

"They're the best. I'm so lucky. We have this big yard, so we just rescue dogs all the time." As soon as she said the words, Andi felt that familiar pang of conscience that told her that maybe the lie had gone a bit too far.

"*All* the time?" Dave asked.

"Uh, I mean, whenever we, uh . . . ," Andi stammered.

She had blown it in a big way this time.

Dave didn't seem to notice, though. He looked at her hopefully. "You know what? Come with me."

Dave led Andi to the back of the pet store, where two dogs, a bulldog and a Border collie, were kept in cages. A sign hanging above them read FREE TO GOOD HOME!

"They're so cute," Andi said.

"We adopt out dogs here, but we can't get anyone to take these guys," Dave explained. "They're not puppies anymore. Everybody wants puppies."

"Tell me about it," Andi said.

"It's too bad. They're great dogs. They're just kind of . . . well, lovably defective." Dave pointed to the bulldog's cage, which was strewn with the wreckage of chew toys, stuffed animals, and various other objects that had once been whole.

"This is Cooper," Dave said, letting the bulldog out. "He's my favorite. I think he's half goat. There's not a substance on Earth he can't chew through."

As Cooper sidled up to Andi, he seemed to also be checking to see if she had anything he might be able to chew.

Dave unlocked the second cage. "And this is Shep. She's got some herding issues." No sooner were the

53

words out of his mouth than Shep bounded out of the cage and circled the two of them.

The shaggy black-and-white Border collie nudged Dave and Andi with her nose, pushing the two of them toward each other. Andi stumbled into Dave's chest, and he reached out his arms to steady her. She was about to thank him but seemed to have trouble finding the words.

Andi realized that she was embarrassed. It probably had something to do with the fact that she thought Dave was supercute and supernice and now she was practically hugging him. She took a step back and cleared her throat.

"Pushy," she said, pointing to Shep.

"I like pushy," Dave said, smiling. Then, realizing that he was still holding onto Andi, he quickly dropped his hands. There was an awkward moment of silence before Andi started talking about the dogs.

"So they've got quirks. They're still adorable."

"Good. I'm glad you think so, because you're going to take them," Dave said.

"What? No!" Andi exclaimed. Where was her little lie taking her?

"The store's owner told me we can't keep them

54

forever and that if I can't find homes for them, they're going to the pound," Dave explained.

"There's no way I can—"

"You're already taking care of some strays . . . what's three more?"

"*Three?*"

"Wait until you see this guy," Dave replied, and called out, "Romeo!"

The oddest-looking little dog she'd ever seen trotted out to meet her. He had a slim body that was mostly hairless except for his head and his paws. His perky ears trailed spiky grayish fur. He reminded Andi of a scrawny punk rocker in fuzzy boots.

"What if you just kept them for a little while?" Dave asked. "I'll pay for food. I've got an employee discount. It's the least I can do."

Andi realized that Dave was making her an offer she couldn't refuse. And as if to confirm that the matter was settled, Romeo barked once, Cooper grunted, and Shep circled around everyone, dogs and humans.

Dave offered to deliver the three dogs and their food supply to their new home. He led Andi to the parking lot in the back of Primary Paws and showed her the Dog Mobile, which was easily the funniest thing Andi had seen all week. It seemed to be what could happen if a dog combined with a truck. This particular truck was Dalmatian inspired, painted entirely white with black spots. It had two black "ears" that hung down from the roof and a shiny black "nose" and pink "tongue" that were stuck to the grille. Lastly, there was a fluffy "tail" attached to the rear bumper.

"Sweet ride," Andi said as she got in.

"It's pretty much a chick magnet," Dave replied, and Andi laughed.

"So, where are we headed?" he asked.

Andi froze. Well, they certainly weren't going to that big fictional house with the big fictional yard that she had invented. She thought fast and came up with another story. "You know, actually, the thing is . . . my parents are kind of out of town for like a month, and we're staying with our Aunt Alice. She's a sweet lady, but she's deathly allergic to dogs, so I kind of had to make other arrangements."

Dave shrugged. "Then where are we going with three dogs and a car full of dog food?"

"Just follow my lead," Andi said.

Heather watched from the pet store as the Dog Mobile pulled out of the parking lot and turned onto the street. Dave and Andi were clearly up to something interesting, and Heather decided it was up to her to find out exactly what that was.

Meanwhile, Bruce had explored the huge hotel, which easily had more than fifty guest rooms. Over the course of the morning he had wandered through most of them as well as several dining rooms, storage areas, and a dusty old kitchen. His greatest find, however, had been what he now called the Machine Room. Every broken-down appliance and piece of electronic equipment was there—all sorts of spare parts, cogs, cranks, washers, ratchets, gears, and much more. It was an inventor's dream come true.

Bruce had spent the past hour in the Machine Room working on a new invention. Every time he threw aside something he didn't need, Georgia would bring it back. This gave him an idea. He would make things to keep the dogs occupied whenever he and Andi couldn't be at the hotel. With the parts he found, he managed to rig together something that looked like a small catapult.

Bruce took the catapult to the second-floor balcony and, sensing she was about to have some fun, Georgia followed. The Boston terrier watched, fascinated, as Bruce pulled back the arm of the catapult and placed a spoon in the basket at the end. As soon as Bruce let go of the arm, it snapped forward and launched the spoon into the air.

Georgia yapped in excitement, scampering off to fetch the spoon. A moment later she returned with the spoon in her mouth and placed it at Bruce's feet. Bruce smiled at Georgia's expectant look. The fetching machine was born!

When Dave and Andi arrived, they walked across the cluttered hotel lobby carrying bags of dog food and supplies. Cooper, Shep, and Romeo lagged behind and began to explore this strange new setting.

"This place is amazing," Dave said. "But do you think it's safe here?"

"Absolutely. We've been poking around for a couple of days and nothing has—" Andi broke off as something flew over the balcony and whacked Dave square in the head.

"Ow!" Dave cried as he fell and dropped his bags.

"What was—?" Andi began, but stopped when she saw Georgia sprint down the stairs and retrieve the spoon that had hit Dave. Georgia scampered back upstairs, and several moments later the spoon hurtled through the air again.

"Hold your fire!" Dave shouted.

Bruce looked over the balcony railing, worried that he and the dogs had been discovered. He breathed a sigh of relief when he saw his sister, but he wasn't sure who was with her.

"Bruce, you remember Dave? From Primary Paws?" Andi said.

"Uh, yeah. Hey." Bruce said, giving his sister a curious look. *What's all this about?* he wondered.

"He needs a place to keep a few dogs, so I thought, we've got a place," she explained as she helped Dave to his feet.

Andi took Dave upstairs, where he marveled at Bruce's makeshift catapult. He kneeled down to take a closer look. "You made this?" he asked.

Bruce nodded.

"Where did you learn to do that?"

"My dad."

"Wouldn't it be easier just to throw it yourself?"

"Oh, it's not close to done," Bruce replied. "When I get it working, the dogs should be able to play fetch even when we're not here."

Dave studied Bruce for a moment. "Can you get me free pay-per-view?"

"No, David, that would be illegal," Bruce said with a wink. He was just about to explain the basics of cable rewiring when an unfamiliar voice rang out.

"Oh, poop!"

Andi, Dave, and Bruce turned to see Heather on the stairs, holding one foot up.

"Literally!" Heather exclaimed. She grabbed a piece of old newspaper from the floor and wiped the bottom of her shoe.

"Uh, sorry about that," Bruce said. "Lenny should know better." At the sound of his name the mastiff whined and slinked away.

"How'd you find us, Heather?" Dave asked.

"I followed the van with the ears and the tail."

"You're not going to tell anyone, are you?" Bruce was worried.

"Why would I tell? I'm going to help you guys," she said.

"Really?" Andi asked.

"I love dogs, and I happen to know a lot about them. There's a lot more to taking care of them than just throwing sticks and feeding them. You need me."

Andi looked at her skeptically. Heather was a bit of an oddball. She couldn't imagine them needing her.

"Okay, pop quiz," Heather said. "Your Great Dane just gobbled his food from his bowl on the floor. Then he starts whining for no reason and breathing hard. What do you do?"

Before anyone could respond, Georgia trotted up to Heather and dropped the spoon at her feet.

"I say she's in," Bruce said.

With a sigh, Andi relented. "Okay, okay. I mean, how much trouble can we get into, right?"

Chapter 7

Bernie sat at his desk holding a file folder. He had a good feeling about the couple who were coming in. All indications were that they were smart, kind, and well-established. They might just turn out to be the perfect parents for Andi and Bruce.

Bernie looked up to see that the prospective parents had arrived. He added "punctual" to his mental list of their good qualities.

"Jeanine, Sean, welcome, thank you for coming in. I've got to tell you, I was really excited when I got your application," Bernie said. He motioned for them to sit down in the chairs opposite his desk.

"Well, we've spent a lot of time talking about this and we're ready," Sean said.

Bernie opened his folder and read over the application once again. "Just to be sure, it says here that you're open to siblings, even older ones."

Jeanine nodded. "I think about families being split apart, and it just breaks my heart."

Bernie was getting more excited by the minute. "Well, you've got great jobs, you're in a great neighborhood . . . I don't want to get too far ahead of myself, but I've got a couple of kids in mind that I think you would love."

Jeanine was overwhelmed with happiness. She dabbed at the tears in her eyes. "Tell us about them."

"Well, the girl's smart as a whip, the boy's some kind of mechanical genius—and it says here that you're an engineer, Sean."

"Will they call me Mommy?" Jeanine asked.

"Well, it's kind of up to them. Some do," Bernie said charitably.

"How soon, on average? It would really mean a lot to me if they would call me Mommy by Thanksgiving."

Bernie sat back in his chair. All the excitement he had a few moments ago took a sudden dive. He saw the desperation in Jeanine's face as he replied, "Again, it's really something that just happens organically. You can't predict it."

"We'll take care of that when we get them home, dear," Sean said, comforting his wife.

"What are their names?" Jeanine asked.

"Well, I mean, there are so many kids who need homes," Bernie answered.

"But you said you had some in mind. We're still getting them, right?"

"Um, the kids I was thinking of are Andi and Bruce. But, you know, adoption is a really long process and—"

"Andi and Bruce," Jeanine said, cutting him off. "Do you think they're too old to change their names?"

At that point Bernie was certain that he couldn't leave Andi and Bruce in the hands of this couple. "Maybe a little," he said curtly.

"Sweetheart, he has to say that," Sean said. "He's a government employee. He can get in trouble if he makes a promise; you know how it is."

Bernie knew that this was not going to work out the way he had hoped. He stood up, signaling that the meeting was over.

"So what's the next step?" Sean asked.

"I'll be in touch," Bernie said. But as soon as they

Andi and Bruce loved their dog, Friday, and would do anything to keep him—even if it meant hiding him in garages and alleys in the neighborhood.

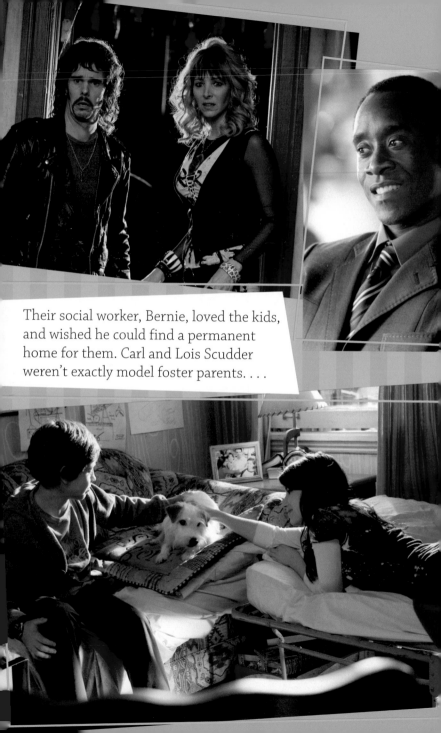

Their social worker, Bernie, loved the kids, and wished he could find a permanent home for them. Carl and Lois Scudder weren't exactly model foster parents. . . .

When Friday found an old abandoned hotel, Andi and Bruce came up with a plan: They would turn it into a safe haven for all the homeless dogs in the neighborhood!

Bruce worked his magic and created gadgets and machines that kept the dogs well fed and entertained in their new home.

Andi and Bruce also had help from Dave and Heather from the pet store, and from Mark the grocery store clerk.

DAVE

HEATHER

MARK

But it was not long before the secret hideout was discovered and the dogs were taken away. Worse, Andi and Bruce had to be separated.

This time Friday rescued *them*—and soon everyone was headed back to the hotel.

Thanks to Bernie, Andi and Bruce were able to turn the hotel into a real Hotel For Dogs, and find a forever family. No one could have asked for a happier ending!

were gone, Bernie tore their file in half and threw it into his trash can.

The next few weeks were a blur for Bruce, Andi, Heather, and Dave. They worked hard around the clock to care for the guests at their fledgling hotel.

Bruce and Andi had the early shift. They woke up at five every morning and walked bleary-eyed to the hotel in order to feed the dogs their breakfast. Once the dogs had eaten, Andi and Bruce took them for their morning walk.

That was easier said than done, however. Between Shep's herding tendencies, Cooper's stubbornness, and Friday's determination to follow any morsel of food no matter how small, they usually ended up in a tangle of arms, legs, tails, and leashes, thrashing about on the sidewalk.

Heather usually took the early-afternoon shift. This happened to be the shift that required the least amount of feeding or dog walking. Heather was free to spend her time painting her nails and encouraging the dogs to find their own inner beauty. She was quite happy with this shift until one afternoon when, in the middle of a relaxing pedicure, she caught Cooper chewing one of her beautiful new strappy sandals.

"Something has to be done!" she complained to Bruce and Andi. "The summer sandal season is upon us, and I've just lost one of my best pairs!"

"I'm sorry, Heather," Andi said, "but you know how it is with dogs. A few shoe casualties are to be expected."

Bruce, however, was a little more sympathetic. After a few days of tinkering, he unveiled his latest invention: a chew-toy vending machine, packed with all kinds of old shoes, boots, and slippers.

As soon as he saw Cooper's reaction to the new machine, Bruce knew he had another satisfied customer. The bulldog eagerly pounced on an old loafer that dropped down into the tray at the press of a button.

Next on Bruce's list was a way to reduce the amount of cleanup. Working with his plans, the others helped Bruce build two rooms. One was a Pee Room. When nature called, dogs would trot up to the fire hydrant in the middle of the room and pee. As they walked away from the hydrant, they would step on a plate in the floor, which would trigger a burst of water from a showerhead above the hydrant. The hydrant was then washed clean and stood ready for the next dog.

The other room was the Poop Room. Bruce found a ramp, which he attached to a long table. He cut a few holes in the table and fitted them with toilet seats. Below the table was a conveyor belt that was lined with a sheet of plastic.

When the dogs did their business, the poop fell through the toilet seat and onto the plastic sheet. The conveyor belt carried the poop over to an area with a hair dryer. The heat from the hair dryer shriveled the plastic sheet beneath the poop, effectively shrink-wrapping it. At the end of the conveyor belt the shrink-wrapped poop dropped into a large trash bag.

It took more than two weeks to finish construction on the Poop Room. When it was finally up and running, the foursome stood back to admire their handiwork.

"That may be the grossest thing I've ever seen," Heather said.

"It's gross," Andi agreed, "but brilliant. And now that you've solved our poop problem, maybe you can use your mighty brain to figure out a way to get us out of those five a.m. feedings."

"Done and done," Bruce replied confidently.

Two days later Bruce rolled over in bed and shielded his eyes from the early-morning sun. He glanced at the empty space on the nightstand where the alarm clock used to sit. Bruce smiled and went back to sleep.

Across town that alarm clock was ringing inside the Hotel Francis Duke. It was attached to another one of Bruce's inventions. The alarm triggered a mechanism that released the dog food down six chutes into six separate bowls. The dogs scampered into the kitchen to enjoy their breakfast. They left after they'd finished eating, all except for Friday.

Friday cocked his head, ears perked as he looked from the alarm clock to the string that attached it to the food machine. It was almost too easy. Friday jumped up and grabbed the string in his jaws. The movement triggered the alarm clock and tripped the switch on the machine, causing food to fall down the chutes into the waiting bowls.

Friday barked happily. He could enjoy six more breakfasts before lunch.

chapter 8

"So my parents are all, 'What do you mean you don't want to go on vacation this summer?'" Heather chatted as she and Andi walked over to the hotel one afternoon. "And I'm like, 'Sun. Sand. Hot guys playing volleyball in teeny tiny bathing suits. It's the same every year. Who needs it?'"

Andi was caught off guard. She had no summer plans. Thinking fast, she told Heather, "Uh, yeah, I know. I mean, I had to tell my parents, 'Look, Europe's been there for two thousand years, it'll be there next year.'"

"Oh, so your parents are back in town?" Heather asked.

"No," Andi lied smoothly. "We were going to fly there,

and they'd fly and meet us from where they are. It was just going to be a big hassle. This is much better."

"You sure? Because Dave and I can hold down the fort while you're gone."

"No, I'd rather be here."

"Cool."

They arrived at the entrance to the hotel and looked around to see if anyone had been following them.

"Coast is clear," Andi said. She and Heather slipped inside. They hadn't noticed the shadow trailing them in the alley.

The girls cut across the lobby and made their way to the Poop Room. Dave was there, checking the bag at the end of the conveyor belt. It was almost full. Someone would have to tie it off and carry it down to the Dumpster.

Just then an unfamiliar voice said, "That is awesome."

Everyone turned to see Mark, the stock boy from Camwell's Market.

"Hey, we just wandered in here and—," Andi said, trying to come up with a story. She couldn't let their secret be exposed. She was cut off by the fetching machine, however, as it launched a tennis ball right at Mark's head. Mark ducked just in time.

Moments later Georgia came barreling into the room to retrieve the tennis ball.

"Don't worry, I'm not going to tell anyone," Mark said. "In fact, if you'll let me, I'd love to help. I just work at the market down the street. I can keep an eye on the fuzz, run interference . . . massage your shoulders," he said, grinning at the girls.

"Easy, tiger," Heather warned.

"We appreciate the offer, but we've got it under control," Dave said. Georgia seemed to disagree. She trotted over to Mark and placed the tennis ball at his feet.

Mark took a step closer to Dave and lowered his voice so that they could have a private conversation, man to man.

"I've got to be honest," Mark whispered. "I'm at a critical point in my social development. Those are two fine-looking women behind you, and you can't date them both. So which one do you have dibs on?"

"Dibs? I don't . . ." Dave's voice trailed off as he looked at Andi.

"Gotcha," Mark said with a wink. He walked over to Heather and introduced himself. "I'm Mark."

"Hi, Mark. You're on poop duty," Heather replied matter-of-factly.

"And so the game begins," Mark said with a grin. "How many dogs are we talking here?"

"Just six," Andi said.

"Actually seven," Bruce corrected. He'd just walked into the room—with a friend.

Andi recognized the large mutt with the choke collar from the brownstone down the street, but she still asked, "What is that?"

"I'm not going to lie to you," Bruce replied. "This is a dog. Actually, this is the newest member of our family—Henry."

Georgia, Friday, and several of the other dogs trotted over to greet Henry.

"Bruce," Andi groaned. Her little brother left out the part where he'd liberated Henry from the mean old man who owned him.

"Honestly, we have plenty of room here. We can take one more," Heather said.

"One more?" Dave laughed. "We have room for ten more."

"Well, we can't just go walking the streets rescuing every stray we find," Andi said.

"Can't we?" Bruce asked.

Everyone exchanged a look. It wasn't such a bad idea.

Chapter 9

A strange thing was happening at the City Pound: Most of the cages were empty. Only a few dogs remained. It was almost as if someone had begun rescuing strays right out from under the noses of city dogcatchers.

It was actually a group of someones.

At the Hotel Francis Duke, Bruce listened to a police scanner tuned to Animal Control's radio frequency. "Okay, guys, we've got a stray at Saint Andrews and Sixth," he radioed his team. "It's only a few minutes from the pound, so hurry."

Bruce studied the large map of the city laid out on a table in front of him. If his intel was correct, then his team should already be in the vicinity. He moved a small plastic dog figurine to the intersection of Saint Andrews and Sixth and waited.

A moment later Dave's voice crackled over the cell phone. "Copy that, Dispatch."

But on the way they spotted two dachshunds by a fence. One was stuck and the other wouldn't leave her. Andi, Dave, and Heather knew they had to help the dogs. Within minutes they were able to free the trapped dachshund—and stopped both of them from being caught by Animal Control.

Once the dachshunds—that they named Viola and Sebastian—were safely in the Dog Mobile, the rescue team headed off to save the stray Bruce had called them about. Arriving at their destination, Andi and Heather intercepted two Animal Control officers who were about to capture a small gray poodle.

"Hello! Sorry to bother you, but could we have a minute of your time?" Heather asked politely.

"We're not interested," one of the men replied.

"We both work on our school newspaper, and we were wondering if we could interview you," Andi explained. She moved in front of the Animal Control officers so that she was blocking their view of the poodle.

Behind the two girls, Mark was dressed in a trench coat. It was his job to get the dog. But he was having a really hard time. The poodle kept backing away from him and finally went to hide behind some trash cans.

Andi and Heather kept trying to distract the officers, but the men were getting very annoyed. Mark realized that he was going to have to resort to plan B. He opened up his trench coat, which he had lined with all sorts of food.

Mark pulled out a chicken leg and waved it. No response. He pulled out a sausage. The poodle continued to ignore him. *Are you kidding me? What dog doesn't like sausage?* he wondered.

Then Mark pulled out a banana. The poodle sniffed, and her ears perked up. Willingly, she walked over to Mark, who quickly scooped her up and stashed her inside his trench coat.

Seeing that the coast was clear, Andi and Heather hurried off—to the relief of the Animal Control officers. The two men looked around for the poodle, but she was gone. All they saw was a teenage boy in a trench coat with a suspicious-looking bulge beneath it.

"What?" Mark asked. "You've never seen a husky kid in a trench coat before?"

Friday helped out in the next rescue mission. Pretending to be a stray, he was able to distract the two very frustrated Animal Control officers, while Dave backed the Dog Mobile up to the Animal Control van. Heather and Andi quickly led all the dogs out of that van and into the Dog Mobile. Mission accomplished!

The kids brought all the dogs to the hotel, but the poodle didn't join her fellow residents until after a major makeover from Heather in the spa.

The hotel's spa was the perfect place to pamper a pooch. The dim lights and CD of nature sounds playing in the background created a relaxing atmosphere for dogs and humans. The room had dog baths and grooming stations, with blow dryers to create the perfect "doggie 'do."

Heather washed and clipped and brushed, and the former stray finally looked like a true poodle, with her fur cropped close along her hindquarters and upper legs but puffy and full around her ankles, chest, and the tip of her tail. And her fur was actually snowy white!

Mark wandered over to Heather, sensing his moment.

"Need a hand?" he offered.

"No," Heather answered. She didn't even bother to look up at him.

"Because I could—"

"No."

"Later, then?"

"No."

"So it's a maybe." That was good enough for Mark. He left Heather with a flirtatious wink and backed away.

Mark wasn't the only one in the room who was smitten. Romeo took one look at the newly groomed poodle and seemed to come down with a bad case of puppy love. She hopped off the grooming station and tossed her hair.

Time seemed to slow down for Romeo as he stared, mouth open, tongue hanging out. He had found his Juliet—and the kids decided that that was the perfect name for the now glamorous poodle.

Heather almost laughed at the look on Romeo's face as Juliet trotted out of the room with her nose in the air. After the briefest of moments Romeo took off after her.

A day later Bruce was making a few adjustments to the poop machine. After he finished tinkering with the conveyor belt, he turned the machine on. The belt chugged forward, carrying poop to the hair dryer, where it was duly shrink-wrapped. Only now, instead of dumping the doo into a waiting trash bag, the conveyor belt carried it to a chute in the wall. The poop fell down the chute and into a Dumpster in the alley. It was a much-needed improvement, and Bruce stood back and looked at his invention with a sense of satisfaction.

The boy thought about how much the hotel had changed over the past couple of weeks. They had started with three dogs, and now they had close to a hundred. With the increase in the hotel's guests, he'd been working hard to come up with new ways to keep them entertained.

First was the Herding Room with his mechanical sheep. He had created the sheep out of old socks, sweaters, and other fluffy material stretched over wire frames. The frames were then attached to old remote-controlled cars. The cars were controlled by a machine that kept them zipping from one end of the room to the other. The result was that Shep and the other working dogs had motorized sheep they could herd whenever they liked.

Just down the hall from the Herding Room was the Car Ride Room. Bruce and the others had propped up old car doors and rolled down the windows. Then they positioned fans in front of the doors. The dogs hopped up onto boxes behind the doors and stuck their heads out of the windows. They could feel the cool breeze blowing through their fur. It was just like a car ride down a highway on a Saturday afternoon.

Bruce was proud of the hotel and everything that he and his friends had accomplished. The bad part was that it had to be a secret, and the secret got bigger and bigger every day. How long could they really keep things quiet?

The Scudders were singing again, and this time they had an audience: two people who were sitting on the living room sofa with their eyes glazed over and their hands clasped tightly in their laps.

Bruce and Andi looked glumly at each other. How much longer would they have to endure this?

Thankfully, Lois soon put a halt to band practice with one of her many complaints. "I don't know," she said. "This song's all about you. It's like the Ballad of Carl. We need a hook. We've got to punch an issue."

"You're harshing my mellow," Carl grumbled.

Lois ignored him. "We need to be the theme song of

an issue . . . where every time it happens, they play us. Like a fire, riots, an election—"

"The plague," Carl suggested.

Just then there was a knock at the front door. Andi and Bruce rushed to answer as if the apartment were on fire. They had never been so excited to see Bernie standing at the door. But before they could say anything, Carl jumped in.

"Bernie, I don't know if you heard, but Lois and I have a gig coming up this weekend. Paid. I'm going to RSVP you and the missus as a yes, right?"

"I'm not sure if I can make it," Bernie answered politely.

"What about that friend of yours who owns the club?"

"He will definitely be there."

"Excellent."

Bruce and Andi cut the conversation short by pulling Bernie out of the apartment and down into the lobby of the Scudders' apartment building.

"So what's the emergency?" Andi asked.

"Not that we don't appreciate you rescuing us from the concert," Bruce said.

"Well, you know how hard I've been trying and . . .

I found the perfect foster parents for you!" Bernie announced.

Andi and Bruce were floored.

"Perfect?" Andi asked.

"Perfect. They had two foster kids who just went off to college, and they're looking for two more. You're going to love them."

"We get to go right now?" Bruce asked.

"They're waiting outside to meet you."

Andi and Bruce looked through the glass doors of the lobby to a car that was parked outside. A nice-looking middle-aged couple sat in the front seat. They smiled and waved.

"The best part is you'll never see Carl and Lois again. In fact, you can pack right now," Bernie said.

Bruce and Andi couldn't believe their luck. They turned back to the stairs, all set to go back to the apartment to pack their things.

"And I'll still be able to see you guys now and then since your new place is only three hours away."

The siblings stopped in their tracks.

"What?" Andi said.

"That far?" Bruce asked.

"Yeah. That's great, right?"

Bruce and Andi exchanged a look.

"I don't know, Bernie. We like the area," Bruce said.

"We've made friends," Andi explained.

"Carl and Lois's singing really grows on you."

Bernie folded his arms across his chest and studied the two of them. They were up to something.

"What is going on here?" he demanded. "You hate Lois and Carl. Do you know what I went through to find these people?"

"We really appreciate that, but I'm afraid we're going to have to pass," Andi said.

"What? Pass? I didn't give you a choice of desserts. These are your new foster parents! Bruce, what do you say?"

Bruce looked at his sister and then turned back to Bernie. "I'd like to stay."

"This opportunity is not going to last, and if things don't work out here, you've probably blown your final shot to stay together. Listen, whatever it is that's going on, it's not better than what I'm offering you right now."

"Sorry," Andi said. She could barely look Bernie in the eye.

"I have no idea what you're up to here. I just hope you know what you're doing." Bernie left the lobby, slamming the door behind him.

Bruce turned to his sister. "We're doing the right thing, right?"

"Yeah, we're going to be fine," Andi answered. She placed a comforting hand on Bruce's shoulder and forced a smile. If only she were convinced by her own words.

Later that afternoon Andi sat on the roof of the hotel with Friday. They had created a roof garden with all sorts of plants and a makeshift fountain. As she looked out at the beautiful view of the city, Andi couldn't stop thinking about what she and Bruce had just done: They had turned down the perfect foster parents. Was it the right decision?

Friday could tell that Andi was upset. He placed a paw on her arm and lifted his muzzle to lick her cheek. Andi smiled. "Thanks, buddy."

"No problem."

Andi jumped. She turned to see Dave standing behind her.

"Sorry," he said. "I didn't mean to scare you."

"That's okay."

Dave put his hands into his pockets and walked over.

"So, are you ever going to tell me why you named him Friday?"

"Someday," Andi said sadly.

"Everything okay?"

"Yeah. Just looking."

"You love it up here, don't you?"

"I'm just guessing it's the kind of view I couldn't have afforded if this place were a real hotel."

Dave chuckled at that. He looked out over the city for a moment, building up his courage. Then he turned back to Andi. "So, hey, listen, you doing anything tomorrow night?"

"Let's see . . . sneak out, serve sixty pounds of kibble, mop up some drool . . . "

"Well, you should take a night off. Friend of mine's having a party. You can meet a bunch of people you'll be going to school with—the key word being *people*."

Suddenly Andi was nervous. Was Dave asking her out on a date?

"I don't know," she said. "I think the hotel has a rule about employee fraternization."

"Not playing by the rules has never really been our problem, has it?"

"You've got a point."

"Great. Where should I pick you up?"

Andi shifted uncomfortably. "You know what? Just tell me where it is and I'll meet you there."

"You're not going to stand me up, are you?"

"I'd never want to do that." They looked at each other for a moment before Dave took a step toward Andi, but he stopped when the sound of Bruce's can-opener dinner bell rang out clearly over the roof's loudspeaker.

"I guess that's dinner," Andi said wistfully.

The dogs gathered in the hotel dining room for dinner, taking their places at a long dining table. Bruce had upgraded his original contraption to accommodate the growing number of dogs. The new feeding machine was a masterwork of ingenuity.

The dog dishes were attached to a belt pulled by an electric toy train. As the train began its journey across the table, it drew the dishes through the feeding machine, which dumped dry kibble and canned food into them. When the train reached the end of the table, the bowls were lined up perfectly in front of each dog. The whole thing was attached to a timer so that it went off automatically. All Bruce and the others had to do was keep the machine loaded with food.

The dogs began their meal as Bruce, Andi, Dave, Heather, and Mark watched from their own small table nearby. Mark leaned over to Heather and whispered in her ear, "Kind of like a dinner date, isn't it?"

"A stranger observing this who had absolutely no idea what was going on might think so, yes," Heather replied, then scooted her chair away from Mark.

Heather turned her attention to Dave, who was busy staring at Andi. *So that's how it is*, Heather thought. She knew a budding romance when she saw one and realized that she had to be grown-up about it.

Heather decided right then and there that she would say something to Dave when she got a chance.

"Dig in," Bruce called from his end of the table. Everyone started to eat.

Of course, no family meal—no matter what kind of family you had—would be complete without a begging dog, and Friday was eager to finish the picture. He hopped down from his spot at the dog's table and headed over to Andi and Bruce. He barked, sat back on his hind legs, and begged for all he was worth. Everyone laughed and tossed scraps of food to him.

Friday chewed happily. It was good to be a dog.

chapter 10

The day of the party had somehow crept up on Andi. She had two hours until she was supposed to meet Dave, and she still didn't have anything to wear to her first real party in a long time. She looked in her bedroom closet and shook her head. In front of her hung two sweaters, a sweatshirt, three ratty T-shirts, and a faded sundress that was way too small. Andi sighed.

"If any cartoon mice or birds are ever going to make me a dress for the ball, this would be a good time," she announced to no one in particular. Not a creature stirred.

Bruce sat on his bed, taking apart a hair dryer. "How long will you be gone?" he asked.

"A few hours, maybe. It's just a party." She tried to sound casual, but her palms were sweating.

"What if something goes wrong at the hotel?" Bruce asked, worried.

"Bruce, you can handle it. You can handle anything. Have you stopped and looked around that place? I could disappear for a week and you could keep it running."

"But you're not going to disappear for a week."

"Of course not. Now if you could just build me a dress, you'd officially be a wizard."

"You should go down to the hotel and check out Room five-oh-two. There's a whole bunch of clothes in there."

Andi was convinced there was nothing her brother didn't know. She grabbed her bag and ran out the door.

Dave checked his watch. The party was in full swing at his friend's apartment, and Andi hadn't showed up yet. He hoped she hadn't changed her mind.

Heather walked up to him. "Look, Dave, I need to talk to you about the situation we find ourselves in," she said seriously.

"Oh-kay . . . ," Dave said slowly, unsure what situation

Heather was referring to, but he had a feeling that she was going to tell him all about it.

"You're torn," Heather began. "Now don't deny it—I can tell. Andi, Heather, Heather, Andi . . . we're both strong, appealing women, and you don't know what to do. I'm going to make it easy for you. I'm going to let you go, because I'm picking up something special between you two."

Dave was a little surprised that his feelings for Andi had been so noticeable—and also surprised that Heather felt something for him. He thought about how to respond.

"Heather, that is . . . amazingly generous," he finally said.

"Be strong. Don't take it too hard," Heather replied as she slapped him on the back.

"I'll try, but listen, I don't even know if she's going to show up to . . ." Dave's voice trailed off as he noticed Andi standing in the doorway.

Andi was flustered as she stepped inside the apartment. She'd spent way too long looking through the clothes in Room 502, but she finally found a vintage dress that fit her perfectly.

And then there was a problem with finding the right

shoes. There weren't any in her size, so she decided to stick with the low-top Chucks she'd been wearing. It wasn't exactly chic, but it was the best she could do on short notice.

Andi knew she was late and had run the last few blocks to the party. By the time she reached the door, she was a bundle of nerves and adrenaline.

Dave didn't seem to notice any of that. He walked right up to her and, after a moment of being at a loss for words, he finally said, "You look . . . wow. Gorgeous."

"What? This old thing?" she joked.

Dave smiled. "Come on, let me introduce you around," he said, guiding her through the crowd of teenagers.

Andi was having a wonderful time. Everyone she'd met so far had been really nice. Dave was great at making introductions, and he was being the perfect date: kind, smart—and incredibly cute in his jeans and sweater.

She was just about ready to call it the perfect evening when she spotted Jason, a neighborhood kid who lived in her building. Uh-oh. Jason was the only one who could blow her cover. He'd seen her with the Scudders.

"Everything okay?" Dave asked. "You look a little pale."

"Yeah, I just need a little fresh air. Care to join me?"

Before Dave could answer, she grabbed him and dragged him toward the door. She wasn't fast enough, however.

"Andi?" Jason said.

"Hey, Jason. You guys have met?" Dave asked.

"Yeah, it's Andi, right?"

"Do I know you?" Andi said, hoping to make a quick escape.

"Yeah, you live in my building. With the Scudders, right?"

"No. I'm over on Oak, but I have one of those faces." Andi's heart was racing. She was desperate to talk her way out of this one.

"No, you live with the Scudders," Jason insisted. "Come on, help me out here. I'm not crazy. They're your foster parents, right? You and your little brother . . . Barry?"

"Bruce?" Heather offered. She'd wandered over to see what was going on. A few other people gathered around. Andi felt as if she were going to sink through the floor.

"Bruce, that's it," Jason said.

"Andi? Is that true?" Dave asked. Andi couldn't look at him.

"What happened to your real parents?" a girl asked.

Heather elbowed her in the side. "Oh, sorry," the girl said quickly.

The mention of her real parents sent Andi into a cold panic. "God, it's no big deal," she said, trying to sound casual. "I guess the Scudders have been foster parents before, but they're also our aunt and uncle, and our parents are traveling in China, so we're just hanging with them. We just call them parents because it's easier than telling this whole boring story."

By now Andi was sweating. Her hands were shaking. She couldn't look any of them in the eye. She knew that they didn't believe a word of it, but she was desperate to make them believe. She was desperate to believe it herself.

Andi turned toward the bar and saw a row of drinks set out on a tray. She grabbed a glass and accidentally bumped the tray. It rocked and teetered dangerously close to the edge of the bar. Andi tried to grab it, but only succeeded in spilling the whole tray of drinks down the front of her dress. It was an absolute nightmare, and the worst part was that she was awake.

Andi looked up to see that the entire party had stopped. Everyone was staring at her, including Dave.

There was only one thing left to do. She ran.

"Andi!" Dave called after her. But Andi didn't stop.

Back at the Scudders' apartment, Bruce was almost ready to head over to the hotel. With Andi and Dave out on their date, it was his turn to load the dog food into the feeding machine. He walked into the bedroom that he shared with Andi, only to find Lois Scudder rummaging through his backpack.

"Hey, that's my personal property!" he said.

"Yeah? Well, what do you call this?" Lois asked. She pulled a hair dryer out of his backpack. "That's *my* personal property. Why are you stealing my hair dryer?"

"It's an old one you don't even use."

"That's really not answering the question, is it?" Lois walked over and grabbed Bruce by the arm. "Come on, mister. You've got some explaining to do."

She marched Bruce into the kitchen, then left to get Carl. Bruce looked around desperately for a means of escape. He was contemplating jumping out of the kitchen window when Lois returned with Carl.

"My wife says you've been ripping us off," Carl

said. "So what else have you stolen from us?"

"Nothing," Bruce answered.

"So you admit you did steal?" Lois questioned him.

"I didn't say that." Bruce chewed his lower lip. He wasn't good at this sort of thing. Andi was usually the one who did the talking. A few more questions from the Scudders and he was going to sing like a canary.

"You might as well tell us the truth. Do you think you're going to outsmart us?" Carl said.

"I'd rather not answer that question," Bruce replied.

"I open my home to you, I open my heart to you, and you steal from me. I'm calling Bernie. I want you both out of my house!" Lois declared.

She picked up the phone and dialed. There was a tense moment of silence while Lois waited for someone to answer the line.

Suddenly the silence was broken by an odd rumbling of sound.

"What is that?" Carl asked.

They listened for a moment longer. As the sound grew louder, it became easier to distinguish. It was the sound of dogs barking and howling.

Bruce swallowed hard and glanced at his watch.

95

He'd missed his chance to load the dog food into the feeding machine. The dogs were howling because they hadn't had their dinner.

"You get Bernie?" Carl asked his wife.

"I'm on hold."

"Tell them it's an emergency. Tell them I'm being stolen from."

"Tell who? I'm. On. Hold," Lois said, annoyed. Then she realized Bruce had escaped.

Friday stared at the empty food dish in front of him. The feeding machine had stopped, but none of the dishes on the long dining table were filled. Not good. Lenny leaned over his dish and whined. Georgia hopped down from the table and scurried off into the hallway. Many of the other dogs barked and paced the room in frustration.

Friday, on the other hand, followed his nose. His sniffed once, twice, and picked up a scent. He jumped down from the table and followed the scent out into the hall. It led him to the kitchen. Several other dogs followed. They began to rummage through some of the open cabinets, looking for scraps of food.

The dogs ran through the hotel, searching for food

and leaving a trail of broken inventions. Friday stood in the middle of the chaos and barked to get his friends to behave, but he was one small dog against a hungry mob. And truth be told, he was pretty hungry too.

Georgia ran down the hall toward one of the guest rooms. There, she found another of Bruce's inventions, a treadmill with a bone dangling from the front. Georgia zeroed in on it.

Little did she know that Henry had also seen the bone. The bigger dog leaped for it, but Georgia was faster. She grasped the bone in her small but powerful jaws and tore it loose. Henry howled and took off, running after her.

Georgia wasn't the only one being chased. Bruce ran as fast as he could toward the hotel. The Scudders were only minutes behind him. He'd circled the block a couple of times, hoping to lose them, but remarkably enough they were still on his trail.

As he approached the hotel, the barking and howling got louder. Bruce was beginning to panic. He had no idea what to expect when he got there.

Georgia and Henry tore through the Car Ride Room,

where Henry crashed into the car doors, toppling them like dominoes. Georgia kept right on running. She cut through the Machine Room, scampering across Bruce's workbench. Henry crashed through after her, knocking over several of Bruce's unfinished inventions. He got caught up in a tangle of spare parts, but that didn't stop him. He kept running, trailing pieces of the broken inventions behind him.

In the hallway some other dogs saw Georgia run by with the bone and decided to join in the chase. Now Georgia had a large pack of dogs on her tail. She scurried through the legs of the scaffolding that the kids used while they were painting the wall. The pack tried to follow but only succeeded in knocking everything over and sending the paint cans flying into the fetching machine. The machine started firing the cans into the air, which sent paint splattering along the hallway— and onto two white pugs.

Bruce walked into the hotel lobby and into the biggest mess he had ever seen. The place looked like it had been ransacked. The dogs swarmed around him, howling and barking. Bruce saw the remains of several of his inventions, as well as torn furniture, scattered about. The paint-covered pugs stumbled by, leaving brightly colored footprints behind them.

Bruce sighed and looked up at the ceiling. *Andi, I can't handle this*, he thought.

Meanwhile, Carl and Lois had seen Bruce disappear into the hotel. They pried open the door at the delivery entrance and let themselves in. The barking and howling got even louder as they found a staircase.

"I can't believe they own a hotel," Carl said.

"Carl, you're an idiot," Lois snapped.

The Scudders made their way past several rooms, some of which were filled with Bruce's inventions. Carl recognized some of the parts that had been used to rig them together.

"I think that's my razor. No wonder my goatee's been looking weird."

Lois rolled her eyes. "They've been robbing us blind," she said. "Why am I not surprised?"

Andi had run from the party toward the hotel. She could hear the commotion inside the hotel from the street. She let herself in and ran straight to the lobby.

"Bruce! Bruce!" she shouted over the sea of howling dogs.

Bruce appeared at the opposite end of the room. He ran toward Andi, holding Georgia in his arms.

"What happened?" she asked.

"Don't ask. What happened to you?" Bruce looked at the giant stain that ran down the front of her dress.

"Don't ask."

They were interrupted by a noise from outside.

"Are those police sirens?" Bruce said. Andi nodded. The two of them sprang into action.

Bruce put the dog down and ran to a fuse box on the wall. He pulled fuses from their sockets and cords from their outlets. The lights began to flicker off in different parts of the building.

Andi grabbed a dog whistle and blew. Neither she nor Bruce could hear the sound, but the dogs heard it immediately. They stopped howling and began to gather around her.

Lois and Carl were wandering on one of the upper floors when the lights went out.

"What was that?" Carl whispered.

"No idea," Lois said.

It was pitch black, and they couldn't see a thing. As they started down the hall again, feeling their way along the walls, a rogue sheep from the Herding Room came whizzing right at them.

"Sh-sh-sh-sheep!" Carl screamed. He grabbed Lois,

and the two of them quickly stumbled out of the way. Then they stood still for a moment, listening.

"Hey, do you hear that?" Carl asked. "It's sirens. That means cops!"

"Great," Lois said. "We can turn them in ourselves. I smell a reward."

"I don't think that's a reward you smell, Lois," Carl noted.

Without warning, the poop machine roared to life! Lois screamed, and the two of them started to run, then tripped over a chew toy—that sent them tumbling headlong down the poop chute.

Andi and Bruce held their breaths as they listened to the police officers clomping through the hotel. There was a small chance that they might be able to pull this off—if the cops didn't find where they were hiding with the dogs.

The siblings were huddled under a huge staircase in the second-floor ballroom with all the dogs packed in beside them. So far so good. They had managed to keep the dogs calm and quiet. *Just a few more minutes and we'll be home free*, Andi thought.

Bruce tensed up as he heard footsteps approach. He saw several flashlight beams dart across the walls.

"Anything in this one?" said one of the officers.

"Nah. Looks empty."

"Better check it out just in case."

In the dim light Andi caught her brother's eye and gave him a weak smile as the footsteps drew closer to their hideout.

Just then Bruce spotted Lenny's expression as the dog realized he was staring at blank walls. "Lenny, no!" Bruce whispered, but it was too late. Lenny threw back his head and howled. The other dogs followed suit and the room erupted into chaos.

Chapter 11

This was the second time Bernie had found himself at the police station on account of Andi and Bruce. He knew they were good kids, so he didn't understand why they insisted on acting like delinquents.

Bernie sighed and turned back to Carl and Lois Scudder. They were a little worse for the wear after having spent the better part of the evening crawling out of a Dumpster of shrink-wrapped poop.

"Look, can't you keep them even for a few nights?" Bernie pleaded. "Just until I can find—"

"Not a chance," Lois retorted. "God knows how much they stole from us. We have a lot of rare and valuable items, and we'll be doing a full inventory and letting you know. This has been an outrage. I'm suing you, I'm suing the state, I'm suing those kids, I'm suing the man who invented shrink-wrap, I'm suing everyone!"

Lois walked off in a huff, dragging Carl with her.

A couple of hours later Bernie had succeeded in getting Andi and Bruce released. As he walked the two of them from the police station, Bernie was clearly upset.

"Are you going to send us to that other house now? With the nice couple?" Bruce asked.

Bernie and Andi exchanged a look. They were both trying hard to protect him.

"Don't worry, Bruce. We'll be fine. I'll take care of it," Andi reassured him. It killed her to see how frightened her little brother was. Andi pulled Bernie aside so that she could speak with him privately. "Come on, Bernie. Help us, please. Bruce needs me. He'll get chewed up out there."

"I'm sorry, Andi. There's nothing left that I can do."

"But you can't separate us. Don't punish him just because I screwed up."

"Andi, it's not up to me." Bernie took her hand, trying to calm her. He could see tears beginning to well up in her eyes. "Listen, the best thing you can do for Bruce right now is to let him have a fresh start."

Before Andi could answer, two other social workers stepped up to separate her from her brother.

"Wait, could I please say one thing to my sister?" Bruce asked. His social worker nodded, and he walked over to Andi. "Look, I'll be okay. Don't worry about me."

Andi closed her eyes. When she opened them again, tears were streaming down her face. "I let you down. I was supposed to keep us together and protect us."

"We had to protect the dogs," Bruce said. "We did exactly what we were supposed to do. If we had to do it over again, I'd do the same thing."

Andi wiped her eyes. She was so proud of her little brother. She hugged him quickly before the social worker led her away.

At the City Pound, Jake couldn't believe his eyes. Van after van of stray dogs were being unloaded in front of the building. He sighed. They were going to take forever to process. The amount of paperwork alone was going to be ridiculous, but he wasn't about to go screwing up the paperwork—that was just not who he was.

Animal Control officers tried to move briskly to lock the dogs up in the cages, but it didn't look like they were going to get to Friday anytime soon. The end of his leash was tied to a bench, but that had never posed a problem for the terrier. Friday ducked his head, flattened his ears, and wriggled his way out of the leash. Then he pushed through the crowd of dogs outside the pound and took off in search of Andi and Bruce.

Bernie was angry and frustrated—more with himself than with the kids. He went back to the hotel and wandered through the rooms, amazed at all the inventions the kids had created to care for the dogs. It was really ingenious the way the contraptions had been designed. Bernie shook his head. It was sad that a place like this had to go to waste. If only there was something he could do about it.

Andi flopped down on the couch in the TV room, where a couple of other girls were watching TV. She had been placed in a foster care facility that felt a little like a home for wayward girls. The food was crappy, and the attendants kept trying to force craft projects on them as if that would keep them out of trouble.

Andi was exhausted and sad. She had no idea where Bruce was, and she was worried about the dogs, Friday in particular. So when a dog-food commercial popped up on the TV screen, she just couldn't handle it.

"Ugh, turn it off," Andi said. She turned away from the television, but the sound of barking continued. "*Please.*"

"I did turn it off," one of the girls said.

Immediately Andi was on her feet. That bark—it sounded familiar. But it couldn't be. She followed the sound of the barking through the building to the front yard. Andi opened the door and sure enough, right there on the sidewalk, was Friday!

The scrappy little terrier ran up to her and jumped into her arms.

"Friday! I can't believe it!" she said, hugging him. She looked up to see Dave waving at her from the Dog Mobile.

Andi wasted no time jumping into the truck. "How did you get him out?" she asked.

"He got himself out. Found me. We went for a drive. Found you," Dave explained.

Andi couldn't have been happier to see them. She was grinning from ear to ear. Then she remembered that the last time she'd seen Dave, he had caught her telling a horrible lie and had watched her spill an entire tray of drinks on herself like an idiot. Her smile quickly faded.

"At this point I think both of you might be better off without me," she said.

"I guess neither one of us is that smart," Dave replied. Something about the way he said it made Andi totally nervous again. She could feel the heat in her cheeks. But she knew it was time she trusted Dave, so she decided to come clean despite the jumpy feeling in her stomach.

"Hold on. You wanted to know why we named him Friday?" Andi asked. She didn't wait for an answer, though. She just kept talking because she knew that if she stopped, she might not be able to finish.

"My parents—my *real* parents—I wish you could've met them. I can't even describe them. You just remember the little things, like how it drove my dad crazy when my hair would get in my eyes and he was always tucking it behind my ear every three seconds. . . . Anyway, they used to take me and Bruce out for a picnic every Friday night. We never canceled. One week we're at a lake, and this little stray gets in our food while we're playing

108

Frisbee. Tiny little puppy ate four people's food! The thing wanted to run away, but it was too full. It waddled like three steps and passed out. What could we do? We had to adopt it. We argued about the name all the way home, and it was my mom who finally came up with the perfect one: Friday."

They sat in silence for a moment.

"That's quite a story," Dave said.

"It's true. Every word."

"I believe you," Dave told her. He smiled and leaned across the seat to pull her into a hug.

Friday hopped up onto the seat and wriggled in between the two of them. Embarrassed, Dave and Andi pulled apart.

"So, any idea where my brother is?" Andi asked.

"I think we can track him down, right, Friday?" Dave said.

Friday barked and wagged his tail.

Bruce had been placed in a large suburban home with five other foster children. It was a nice enough place, but he was absolutely miserable. He was sitting on the front porch when he saw the Dog Mobile cruise down the street. He immediately grabbed his backpack and headed for the Dog Mobile.

"So what's the plan?" Bruce asked, once he was inside the truck.

"The dogs have less than a day left. We've got to get them out of the pound right now," Andi said.

"That's really more of a goal than a plan," Bruce pointed out.

"Dave found a no-kill shelter outside the city. If we can get them out of the pound and over the county line, they're home free."

"And then what happens to us?"

"It's . . . it's not going to be good, Bruce. We're going to get in more trouble than we've ever been in, but at least we don't have to let all those dogs die."

Bruce nodded. "It's what we're supposed to do."

The Dog Mobile was parked just across the street from the City Pound. Andi and Dave peered through the windshield, spotting Heather and Bruce in position just outside the building. Friday jumped onto the dashboard to get a better view. As soon as he spotted the pound, he began to growl.

"We ready?" Andi asked.

"I say let's go," Mark said from the back of the truck. He was dressed from head to toe in camouflage, prepared for a serious operation. "I've got sausage!"

"Oh, great," Dave said sarcastically.

Across the street, Heather saw Andi give the thumbs-up sign from the Dog Mobile. It was time to set the plan in motion. She ran up to a window on the side of the building and pounded on the glass.

"Fire!" she yelled.

Inside the building Jake sat at the front desk playing video games. He jumped when he heard someone pounding on the glass.

"Fire!" Heather said again. "Hello! When a young girl screams for help and says 'fire,' you're supposed to get moving!"

Jake jumped up from the desk, grabbed the fire extinguisher from the wall, and ran out the front door. Heather was waiting for him. "Over there!" she pointed, directing him around the corner.

As soon as Jake was out of sight, Heather motioned to the others. Andi, Bruce, and Friday leaped out of the Dog Mobile and made a break for the pound.

Jake ran down to the corner and looked around.

There was no fire in sight. He turned back just in time to see several kids run into the pound.

"Hey!" he yelled. But by the time he reached the front doors of the pound, they were locked. Andi had jammed a capture stick through the door handles, wedging the doors shut.

Jake pounded the doors in frustration.

"I wouldn't worry about it," Heather said. "Just a couple of kids eager to adopt, I'm sure."

Jake glared at her and ran around the side of the building.

Heather spoke quickly into her cell phone. "Okay, guys, get over here."

Mark's voice crackled through the receiver. "We're rigging the meat. Repeat. We are rigging the—hey!"

A moment later Dave's voice sounded over the line. "We'll be right there!" he answered.

Inside the pound Bruce and Andi were busy unlocking cages. A large crowd of dogs was forming in their wake. Some of them followed Bruce and Andi, while others simply wandered. It was going to be difficult to lead them all out of the building in one large group.

Andi saw Shep, the Border collie, in one of the cages. She ran over and unlocked it.

"This is your time, girl. Let's round 'em up and get 'em out of here. Go, go!" Andi said.

Shep sprang from her cage, barking excitedly. She began herding the dogs toward the back door.

"That's it; the cages are empty!" Bruce called.

"Great. Let's get out of here!"

The two of them ran for the exit, followed by the huge pack of dogs, but Jake jumped out and blocked their path. He'd found his way in through an unlocked side door just in time to put a stop to the jail break. He grabbed a capture stick from the wall and planted his feet in front of the exit.

"What do you think you're doing? No one's going anywhere!" Jake said, waving the stick. Andi and Bruce looked at each other. They'd come too close to fail now.

Henry agreed. The failed guard dog set his teeth in a menacing snarl. He faced off with Jake, who raised the capture stick, hoping it would hold off the growling Henry. No problem—Henry grabbed the stick in his teeth, snapped it in two, and tossed it aside. Jake scrambled to get away from the angry mutt. He looked around for some place to run, but everywhere he turned, he was surrounded by dogs. Henry barked viciously, moving closer.

Jake saw only one option. He crawled into a cage and shut the door, effectively sealing Henry out. Unfortunately, he also locked himself in. Any hope for escape vanished when Jake saw one of the freed dogs taking off with his keys in its mouth.

Satisfied that the Jake problem was solved, Henry trotted toward Bruce and Andi, and they ran for the door with the pack of dogs in tow.

At the rear entrance of the pound, Heather spoke urgently into her cell phone: "Back her up, boys."

Dave had the doors of the Dog Mobile open. Heather could see Mark waving to her in his goofy camouflage outfit. She was just about to jump into the truck when someone grabbed her by the arm.

"You're not going anywhere!" said an angry Animal Control officer.

As Heather struggled to free herself, Mark knew what he had to do. He would sacrifice himself for the woman he loved . . . or at least, really liked.

Mark dived out of the truck and tackled the Animal Control officer. "Save yourself!" he cried.

Heather managed to break free just as the back doors to the pound flew open and Bruce and Andi came running toward her at the head of a herd of dogs.

Heather jumped into the truck, followed by Bruce and Andi. Dave pulled away but not before Heather could call out, "Mark?"

"Yeah?"

"Thank you."

"We'll always have the Poop Room!" Mark said. He watched Heather and the Dog Mobile drive off.

"Be careful, Bruce!" Andi called. Her brother was hanging from the Dog Mobile, dangling meat out of the back doors. The pack of dogs followed the van, with Friday in the lead, closest to the food, of course. Five more minutes and they would have the dogs safely across the county line. Andi crossed her fingers, hoping that this crazy plan of theirs would succeed.

Dave made a left, heading for the city limit. The dogs, on the other hand, went right.

"Problem!" Bruce shouted from the back of the truck. "They just went the other way!"

"What?" Andi said. She made her way to the back of the truck to stand beside Bruce. Sure enough, the dogs had split off and gone in the opposite direction. "Where are they going?"

Bruce thought a moment. Then it dawned on him. "Home. They're going home."

It didn't take long for the city police to notice a pack of dogs on the move. Within a matter of minutes the dogs had the cops on their collective tail. It was an unlikely procession, and the longer it went on, the greater the number of people who joined the pursuit. Animal Control followed the cops who followed the dogs. The local news media followed Animal Control, who followed the cops, who followed the dogs. Bringing up the rear of the procession was the Dog Mobile, which fought its way through traffic toward the hotel.

By the time Andi, Bruce, Dave, and Heather reached the hotel, the police had arrived. And as they made their way into the lobby, they were surprised to see that a large crowd had gathered—people were petting and playing with the dogs!

The four kids pushed their way through the crowd to where Jake and the team of Animal Control officers were talking to the police.

"Nothing to be upset about, Officer. Animal Control is on the scene," Jake said. Officer Mike stared at him, unimpressed.

"If you'll just let us do our job, we'll have these

dangerous canines rounded up and out of your hair in no time," added an Animal Control officer.

"No, wait! Don't let them have the dogs!" Andi yelled.

"You again? Didn't I bust you and your brother for arts and crafts?" Officer Mike asked.

"Please . . . those dogs belong to us," she pleaded.

"They're our family," Bruce added.

"And we're not going to let these coverall-wearing goons take them!" Heather said, pointing to the Animal Control squad. "You can put that in your report!"

"Officer, if you'll kindly arrest these young felons, we've got work to do," Jake said, before nodding to one of the Animal Control officers, who stooped down and picked up the nearest dog by the scruff of the neck. It was Friday. He whimpered.

"Hey, put him down!" Andi cried. She ran straight toward Jake.

"Slow down there, miss," said Officer Mike. He grabbed Andi by the arm, and then Dave jumped into the fray.

"Let her go!" he shouted. A small scuffle broke out, but it ended abruptly as the sound of one voice rose above the crowd.

"STOP!"

Everyone turned to see who had yelled out. There, at the top of the lobby stairs, stood Bernie.

"Okay, now, who are you?" said Officer Mike.

Bernie held up a badge. "Bernie Wilkins, Social Services."

Officer Mike thought about that for a second and then turned back to rounding up the kids.

"I said STOP!" Bernie shouted. "You think you could take one minute to hear me out before you take kids to jail and kill innocent dogs? And you might want to make sure Channel Four gets your answer."

Officer Mike turned to see a news camera pointed right at him. "Well, I guess there's no reason not to hear all sides," he said, smiling into the camera.

"Look, I'm responsible for these kids," Bernie said. "And I know what they did was wrong. It's breaking and entering, it's trespassing, it's theft . . . and I just wish I had the guts to do what they did."

Bruce and Andi looked at each other. Where was Bernie going with this?

"I've been trying to find homes for children for fifteen years, and most of the time I'm not very successful. But these kids did what I couldn't. They didn't make excuses or get frustrated by the system.

They went out and saved everyone."

Bernie held up a large book with the letters HFD on the cover. It was the hotel guest register. He opened the book and began to read.

"Madison, August third, found hiding in a backyard after family moved away and left her behind. Chelsea, July twenty-fifth, lost leg in an accident, owner didn't pay bill. Abandoned her at the vet. Rocky, Harley, Coco, living together in the woods near a dump . . . "

As Bernie read the dogs' names from the book, each of them began to move through the crowd toward him. They gathered on the steps and sat watching him with their tails thumping the floor.

"Ginger . . . Juliet . . . Henry . . . Romeo . . . ," Bernie continued to read. "Cooper . . . Shep . . . George." They all came forward, all except for George. "George?" Bernie said again.

"Actually, it's Georgia," Andi corrected him.

"And don't forget Lenny," Bruce said. The mastiff and the Boston terrier trotted through the crowd and sat down at Bernie's feet.

"Looks like these guys are the original guests of this Hotel . . . For Dogs," Bernie said. "No one turned away that needed a home. No one turned away that needed a family. And now, are we really going to turn our backs on them?"

A news reporter walked over to Officer Mike.

"They don't look like a bunch of mangy strays, Officer," she said. "You don't mind if we take a look upstairs, do you? I think it's in the public's best interest."

Officer Mike nodded and ordered his fellow officers to stand aside. The crowd followed the news reporter and camera crew up the lobby stairs. Even the guys from Animal Control decided to look around.

Bruce scooped Friday up into his arms, and Andi breathed a huge sigh of relief. Somehow they had managed to pull this whole thing off.

Dave turned to Andi. "You did great," he said.

"You don't think I was too pushy?" she asked.

"I like pushy," he replied. Before Andi could say another word, Dave leaned in to kiss her.

Bruce smiled and covered Friday's eyes.

They were still kissing moments later when Bernie walked up and tapped Dave on the shoulder. He and Andi sprang apart.

"You think I could have a moment?" Bernie asked.

"Yes, sir," Dave said, and stepped aside.

Andi was blushing furiously, and it took her a moment to pull herself together. When she finally looked up at Bernie, his wife, Carol, had joined them.

"You kids are heroes. You should be proud," Carol congratulated them.

"Thanks," Andi and Bruce said in unison.

Bernie looked from Andi to Bruce and back again. His expression was somber.

"So, kids, the bad news in all this is that I still haven't been able to find you a new foster family."

"That's okay, Bernie. We know you did your best," Andi said.

"Actually, I found you some real parents. They want to adopt you."

"Adopt?" Andi asked. She and Bruce looked at each other, afraid to get their hopes up.

"The mom is awesome," Bernie began with a sidelong glance at his wife. "She's a teacher, so I know she's great with kids."

"And the dad," Carol said, "well, he can't cook to save his life, he shouts at football games like the players can hear him—"

"Now, wait just a minute," Bernie interrupted. He and Carol exchanged a glance and burst out laughing.

121

By now it was clear to Bruce and Andi who their new parents were going to be, and they couldn't have been happier. They hugged Bernie and Carol and whooped in delight.

Just then Friday barked, reminding Andi of something very important. "So these new parents of ours . . . do they like dogs?" she asked.

"We love dogs!" Carol exclaimed.

Friday barked again. That was music to his ears.

epilogue

Several months later Heather beamed with pride as she led yet another couple through the front doors of the hotel.

"Thank you so much for calling about adopting the dachshunds. Allow me to welcome you to the Hotel For Dogs."

The couple followed Heather into the newly renovated lobby. It was bright and freshly painted, with brand new furnishings and, of course, dogs. They lounged on chairs and dog beds and enjoyed the treats that were stashed in bowls all over the room.

Dave sat at the registration desk, updating the

guest ledger. He ran his finger down the lists of dogs' names and stamped the word "adopted" next to several of them.

Heather waved to Dave as she walked past. He smiled at her and tossed treats to Lenny and Georgia, who sat patiently by the desk dressed as bellhops.

"You'll note that this is a hotel of dogs, by dogs, and for dogs. Many of our original guests hold jobs here," Heather explained.

She waved to Henry, and the big mutt lumbered forward to meet her. He approached the couple behind her and sniffed them thoroughly.

"Meet our sophisticated security system," Heather said. After a moment Henry barked. "All clear."

She continued the tour, leading the couple through the puppy nursery, where Romeo and Juliet sat with their odd-looking but nonetheless adorable puppies. Mark winked at Heather from the opposite end of the room where he was finalizing a puppy adoption. She smiled at him and waved back.

Heather led the couple back to the lobby.

"Finally, you'll see that we have a variety of activities designed to amuse every dog." She directed their attention toward the stairs, where Bruce's latest invention, the Stroll-a-Coaster, drifted by. It looked just like a ski lift for dogs. Two guests floated past, seated in little baskets.

"This place is wonderful," the couple remarked.

"Wait until you see the dachshunds," Heather replied.

On the rooftop garden, Andi and Bruce were looking out over the city.

"What do you think of the new parents?" Andi asked her brother.

"I don't think we're going to have any luck complaining to our social worker, so we might as well just tough it out," Bruce replied.

"Okay, who ordered well-done?" Bernie asked. Bruce and Andi turned to see him standing over a grill, flipping hamburgers. "Because they're *all* well-done."

Carol stood beside her husband, holding a plate of buns. "Don't say I didn't warn you," she whispered to the kids.

"Hey! I heard that!" Bernie said.

"It's okay. We like to think of him as being lovably defective," Andi explained.

The "lovably defective" Bernie Wilkins flipped a burger into the air. It hung there for a moment before gravity pulled it back toward the grill. Bernie threw out his spatula to catch it, but he fumbled instead, knocking the burger over the edge and into the waiting jaws of a white Jack Russell terrier with brown ears and a nose for food.

Friday carried the burger over to his BONE, SWEET BONE pillow and sat down to enjoy his meal. It wasn't a hot dog, but it would do.

Besides, he'd take a family over a hot dog any day.